STORIES FROM
....
SARATCHANDRA

Saratchandra Chattopadhyay (1876–1938) was one of the most prolific novelists and short story writers from Bengal in the early twentieth century. Among his novels, his most notable works include *Baikunther Will, Pather Dabi, Devdas* and *Srikanta*; stories such as 'Mejdidi' and 'Mohesh' rank among the most loved. Saratchandra's powerful portrayals of human, economic and social distress, colonialism, middle-class lives and the rural world are still widely read, translated and have been adapted into films.

Anindita Mukhopadhyay teaches History in the University of Hyderabad and was formerly fellow at the Indian Institute of Advanced Study, Shimla. She completed her graduation from Presidency College, Calcutta University, Kolkata, her Masters and M.Phil. from Jawaharlal Nehru University, New Delhi, and her Doctoral dissertation from the School of Oriental and African Studies, London. She has translated Rabindranath Tagore's 'Sesher Kobita'—*The Last Poem* (2007), and authored *Behind the Mask: The Cultural Definition of the Legal Subject* (2013).

STORIES FROM
SARATCHANDRA

· ·

INNOCENCE AND REALITY

· ·

SARATCHANDRA CHATTOPADHYAY

Translated by
Anindita Mukhopadhyay

RUPA

Published by
Rupa Publications India Pvt. Ltd 2018
7/16, Ansari Road, Daryaganj
New Delhi 110002

Sales centres:
Allahabad Bengaluru Chennai
Hyderabad Jaipur Kathmandu
Kolkata Mumbai

Translation Copyright © Anindita Mukhopadhyay 2018
Introduction Copyright © Anindita Mukhopadhyay

ISBN: 978-81-291-5040-0

First impression 2018

10 9 8 7 6 5 4 3 2 1

Printed at Thomson Press India Ltd. Faridabad

To Esha, Kaustav and Professor Tuteja—
in friendship

CONTENTS

TRANSLATOR'S NOTE

The translations of Saratchandra's short stories have tried
to render the author's unique style—satirical, conversational,
lyrical—and yet all of it delivered with great ease. However,
it has been impossible to translate Saratchandra's complete
mastery of local dialects. I have also taken some liberties in
interpreting Saratchandra's use of the verb 'said' (*bolilo, bolilen*) in
conversations, in accordance with their tonal pitch. Thus, instead
of using the flat 'said', I have used 'told', 'stated', 'accused',
'said sharply', demanded', 'denied' and other connected verbs.
This strategy, at least, retains the cadence of the conversations.
Further, I felt that Saratchandra's refusal to be pinned down by
accurate temporal measurements had to be respected however
cumbersome 'ten to twelve' or 'fifty to sixty' may sound. It
is therefore nearly always, 'I was perhaps ten to twelve years
old' or 'fifty to sixty years ago…'. This anecdotal reference to
time reflects a flexible frame of reference which I have not
flattened to 'twelve', or 'sixty'. I felt that there had to be a
reason for such a repeated use of an approximation of time.
It might be due to a conversational style of narration clearly
manifest in this collection of short stories. It could even be a
form of cultural resistance to the colonial culture's insistence

on temporal precision. It might also be a combination of both (maybe Saratchandra had other reasons too). Perhaps such an approximate use came with Saratchandra's anecdotal style—reinforced by catchy phrases like, 'Let it go' (*Jak ge*) when he had very deliberately taken a detour while telling a story, and wanted to return to the main narrative.

Further, forms of address are peculiar to the Bengali language. The parents can address the daughter as 'maa' while the same form of address is used by the daughter or son for the mother. The parents can address the son as 'baba' while this is also the formal address for the father. I have retained this cultural specificity while translating conversations. I have attempted no translation of certain words like 'babu', 'chhotobabu', 'Bada Miyan', 'Chhota Miyan', 'thakur', 'moshai','thakurmoshai','thakur mohashoyey', for these are all honorifics, and used as is, they add to the cadence of the Bengali language.

Further, the 'ch' is palatal/talavya. The English phonetic pronunciation will follow 'ch' as in 'church' respectively. The hard palatal with more breath expelled on its pronunciation will use—'chh' as in Bochhor.

The short A will be spelt with as 'a' and the long Ā will be spelt as 'aa', LĀLU will be spelt as Laalu and so on.

Sarat Chandra and Hemendra Kumar are double-barreled names but have been fused into one.

INTRODUCTION

I

As his life was drawing to a close, Saratchandra Chattopadhyay (1876–1938), at a public felicitation on his 57th birthday, summed up his literary career in a characteristic manner—half earnestly, half humbly:

> I have received much more than my share of gifts from the people of my country for whatever little service I have rendered to literature.
>
> I remember especially on this day, how little of this I can truly claim, and what a big debt I owe. This huge debt is not something I owe only to the literary greats who have preceded me. Those who have given their all to this world, and got nothing in return—the deprived, the weak, the oppressed—though they are human beings, their tears have never counted in the eyes of other people; who could never imagine that in their sad, unfortunate lives, they could lay claim to anything that was spread out before them: to these human beings my debt is also very high. Their pain has unlocked my lips, they have

sent me to the people to carry their plaint. I have seen injustice, oppression: I have even seen objective justice meted out to them—which is intolerable...

I know...spring comes full of beauty and wealth. ...but the frame on which my eyes remained fixed did not permit them entry. ... The moment one looks into my writing, this poverty is starkly visible. But what I could not feel in my heart, I could not serve up as soulless offerings dressed up in pretty words... There are also other things, things which I do not understand, and so I have never written about them ... And thus, my service to literature has remained narrow and my themes, instead of casting their nets far and wide, are limited within tight, tiny parameters. But I can certainly claim that I have not written what I have not felt, and not being dishonest is enough for me (*satyabhrashta*).[1]

A younger contemporary of Saratchandra, Hemendrakumar Roy, talks of Saratchandra's entry into the literary field due to the constant prodding and pushing by friends who were providentially editing literary journals, and were on the lookout for talented writers. The first story, 'Bododidi' (Elder Sister) was published in Saraladebi Choudhurani's journal, *Bhaarati*, without Saratchandra's knowledge.

Saratchandra had certainly addressed the central lack in

---

[1]This speech was in response to the celebration of Saratchandra's 57th birthday in 1933, second Aswin of 1339 in the Bengali calendar, in Calcutta's Town Hall. From Sukumar Sen (ed.), *Sulabh Sarat Samagra* (henceforth *SSS*), Vol. 2, Kolkata: Ananda Publishers, 1993, p. 2217. I have retained the word 'satyabhrashta' in the quote translated here since it is a strong word used by Saratchandra and conveys a Gandhian influence on his ethics as a writer.

middle-class perspective in which, till he partially redressed such a skewed social vision, the voices and the faces of the oppressed remained generally unheard and invisible. He had made the middle class (upper and lower) his very own turf, in critique and in panegyrics. As he was very well acquainted with the rural communities in the villages—the well-off, the rich, the poor and the marginalized groups—he drew the pith of his stories from his own personal exposure to them.[2] With the exception of two stories, 'Mohesh' and 'Abhaagi's Heaven' ('Abhaagir Swarga'), both included in this collection, it is Saratchandra's middle-class protagonists who are the vectors of social change and quiet rebellion. Perhaps initially, they blend in with their environment, but under the compulsion of a cathartic moment, their mental worlds shift, change and reconfigure—which then run against standard perceptions of social codes and behaviour.

This collection of short stories, for the convenience of the reader, has been divided into two sets. The first set of stories is around Saratchandra's perceptions of childhood. It is important to note that girlhood is strictly absent from these stories. The reasons are clear. First of all, girlhood was visible only through familial lenses, and remained confined by and largely within the domestic sphere of households. Then again, girls between ten and twelve were considered too old to roam around without adult supervision, and this is noticeable even within Saratchandra's novels and stories. The girls of very

---

[2]'My home is in a Bengal village; I do not think even my greatest enemy would accuse me of not having any knowledge of rural Bengal. I have gone to each and every home...', in 'The Rebellion of the Youth' ('Taruner Bidroha'), in SSS, Vol.2, p. 1955.

educated families were exceptions but, by and large, there was not much difference between urban and rural divides on this social restriction on the girl child.[3]

Further, Saratchandra understood the 'child' as a marginalized, invisible and vulnerable member of the society. Though *Srikanta*, as a novel, could not be included in this collection, the first three episodes in Part I of *Srikanta* depict a regimented world of children, where power emanated from the male authority in the household and flowed through the older brothers: the younger children were supervised by these fairly tyrannical seniors who took advantage of the powerlessness of these much-younger cousins. Within all these stories, there is a social context of power and domination within the familial affect, which was a social reality, despite being occasionally invisible in the frame of a story. In the three *Laalu* stories, the 'father' and all father figures have an irresistible field of power. Old matriarchs are equally awe-inspiring in stories like 'A Day's Tale From Some Fifty Years Ago' ('Bochhor Ponchaash Purber Ekta Diner Kaahini') and 'The Child-snatchers' ('Chheley-dhora').

As these were joint families, there were a large number of children—young and old. Within the family, then, there were collective memories of oppression and injustice, which cohered the bonds of affect and friendship. Children from poorer kin groups also found place within this familial community. Saratchandra's stories—and *Srikanta* is no exception—highlight the extended family as the 'buffer zone' between the core family, the impoverished relatives and the world. Srikanta, the

---

[3]Ruby Lal, *Coming of Age in Nineteenth-Century India: The Girl Child and the Act of Playfulness*, New Delhi: Cambridge University Press, 2013.

Saratchandra Chattopadhyay

rebellious protagonist, an autobiographical reflection of the author himself,[4] was also a young boy staying in a relative's house for his education, so that he could grow up to be a successful adult. But his friendship with Indranath, an unsuitable companion, jeopardized this natural progression materially:

> People who know me will say, 'That wasn't a wise move, boy! In order to get a good education, you left the village and had to stay with relatives. Why did you seek his company...
>
> Only the Omniscient One will be able to say "why", out of so many persons, my heart and mind yearned only for the company of such a never-do-well...[5]

II

Saratchandra did not create a Never-never Land for his young readers, he did not attempt to deflect their imagination to a world where all worldly rules—social, temporal, or physical—were suspended. His young protagonists inhabited a world of rigid hierarchy and authority, of social relations, of a familiar everydayness. However, he represented the familiar through deeply personalized optic shifts, through which the unfamiliar could be vaguely glimpsed. Some of his young protagonists were precocious; they flouted every rule in the calendar, and yet possessed an instinctive and commonsensical understanding of human sympathy and affect. These stories for children were written between 1935–37 (1342–44 BS) when he was already

---

[4]Meenakshi Mukherjee, *Realism and Reality: The Novel and Society in India*, Delhi: Oxford University Press, [1985] 1994.

[5]In *SSS*, Vol. 1, p. 270.

beginning to feel the effects of disease—the Emperor of all Diseases—but which was, as yet undiagnosed. His protagonists, therefore, came out of a lifetime of cogitation about the virtues, and even the vices, that shaped the perceptions of the young and made them grow into compassionate and open-minded adults.

Saratchandra was not interested in creating worthy 'citizens', in putting together stories that would place unbeatable, invincible protagonists before the imagination of young readers. He did not allow his protagonists to show the way to 'achievement-oriented masculinities', who hunted out adventures for the sake of adventures, or who celebrated the glory of muscles and masculine will. However, there is a clear note struck for the spirit of 'boyhood' and 'boyish mischief'. Girlhood is conspicuous by its absence. Saratchandra's stories have time and again been held together by the strong hand of a woman protagonist, but a child's indomitable spirit of mischief and fun is nowhere visible within a girl. The strong women seem to come from nowhere—as they are never children (with the mild exception of *Devdas*'s Parvati). Rabindranath Tagore had created an unforgettable girl child, Mrinmoyee, in his short story 'Samapti',[6] but had weaned her from her girlhood by turning her into a woman who surrenders her mischief-loving days for the greater fulfilment of wifehood! It is here that we clearly see Saratchandra to be deeply embedded in middle-class patriarchy. He could think of a principled, ethical and humane female mind, razor-sharp and agile, and therefore a rebellious woman struggling against the oppressive forces of the social-within-the-familial. But his imagination baulked at

---

[6]Rabindranath Tagore, *Rabindra Rachanabali*, *Sulabh Sanskaran* on 125th Birth Anniversary, Vol. 9, Kolkata: Vishwabharati, 1995, pp. 385–89.

the idea of the female body, bounding along in mischievous freedom, in joyous, unwomanly abandon.

Saratchandra's male child protagonists are wayward, and there is a constant leitmotif in his novels and short stories about rebellious boys refusing to be schooled. Responsibilities and moral strength for the right kind of behaviour is also absent. In fact, in *Srikanta* there is a clear satire on that 'good' boy, the core of the bhadralok identity: 'Somehow I cannot help feeling that when God draws somebody's curiosity towards the vast, fascinating and strange world he has created, he also does not provide too many opportunities to him to pass examinations and become a "good boy".'[7]

Hemendrakumar Roy, himself the creator of four pairs of ultra-masculine adventure-seekers and detectives in the backdrop of colonial Bengal of the early twentieth century, states that Saratchandra's collection of short stories for children did not have too many takers among the young readers. 'I sometimes hear rumours about the demand for children's books in the market. Perhaps for this reason many peep into the children's playroom out of curiosity. But the results are not satisfactory. There is a book of this variety by Saratchandra—I had titled it *Tales from Childhood* (Chhelebaelaar Golpo). This book did not fare as well (in the market) as Saratchandra's other books. Children do not respond to a style written for adults.'[8]

However, it is perhaps important to note that Saratchandra did not create his youthful protagonists in the image of the established pattern of Western icons constructed by Sir Arthur

---

[7] *Srikanta*, Part One, in *SSS*, Vol. 1, p. 268.
[8] In Geeta Dutta (ed.), *Hemendrakumar Roy Rachanabali*, Vol. 4, Kolkata: Asia Publishing House, [1985] 2010, p. 262.

Conan Doyle like Sherlock Holmes and Dr Watson, or boy's adventure stories by the same author, like *The Lost World*. Hemendrakumar Roy's doubles—Bimal, a combination of brain and brawn, and Kumar, his fearless sidekick, as the adventure seekers, and Jayanta, a six-and-a-half foot giant with amazing powers of detection and physical endurance, with his friend Manik—are clear copycat versions of Western masculine dreamboats.

A Laalu or an Indranath does not play out colonial fantasies, though they are still fantasies of masculinity—fearless, humane, spirited, and detached about death. Moreover, they are not college graduates, capable of decoding cartographical secrets relating to unseen, undiscovered and uncharted locations. They are, on the contrary, school dropouts, fully embedded in an indigenous sociopolitical structure; for them, an ultimate act of rebellion was to disappear after accepting *sannyas*.[9] Because they are implanted in 'real' worlds, there are obvious points of reference which might have triggered anxieties in conformable and comfortable middle-class young readers. After all, treasure hunting and decoding secret cyphers, and being chased by inevitable villains, encompass the colonial chronotopicity played out in the imagination of young Bengali readers.[10] These stories do not have any real referents within the reader's imagination,

---

[9] *Sannyas* is the stage of life where one left one's family and the society as a mark of giving up worldly desires. In an autobiographical aside, I can testify to even anglicized children's reaction to Saratchandra's stories in this collection—for it was our Bengali rapid-reader in Class VII. 'Childhood Memories' ('Balyo-Smriti') had been omitted, as the protagonist was considered unsuitable for schools. Still, the stories considered suitable were so funny, we could barely read the lines through laughter.

[10] Sibaji Bandopadhyay, *'East' Meeting 'West': A Note on Colonial Chronotopicity*, DSA Programme, Comparative Literature, Jadavpur University, Kolkata.

and certainly not within the social context. Challenging the rite of animal sacrifice, or trudging with a hearse to the cremation grounds at the dead of night are within the realm of the 'doable' and thus the reader is in a slippery domain of self-referentiality, and therefore, uncomfortable. Moreover, even the recognizable colonial product, complete with great abilities to pass examinations, possessing loads of factual information culled from textbooks, and the desire to surprise countrified yokels with such superiority, is too close to the real-life reader for comfort. Indranath's maternal cousin, Notun-da, is one such recognizable caricature.[11]

> Notun-da twisted up his face, and declared, 'What do you know? We are from Darjipaadaa (in Kolkata), we do not fear even Yama. But we do not enter the *chholotolok*'s[12] dirty localities—just the smell from those fellows make us sick.'[13]

Saratchandra draws on both models for his stories, with some variations in degrees of anglicization. Notun-da and others of his ilk are certainly in the extreme mode, but there are also more indigenous versions of the 'good boy'. This is the variety that is invoked in 'A Day's Tale From Some Fifty Years Ago', as a general archetype of the conformist kind, with a normal schoolchild's urge to play truant, but with no desire to part company with books on a permanent basis. Moreover, the child protagonist also has the trusting faith in the colonial state's power to punish, a might he invokes in all innocence,

---

[11] *Srikanta*, Part One, in *SSS*, Vol. 1, p. 293.

[12] *Chhotolok* refers to people from the lower strata of the society, ones without money, class or even education.

[13] *Srikanta*, Part One, in *SSS*, Vol. 1, p. 295.

and therefore all the more tellingly does he re-establish the acute invasion the colonial state had made into the minds of the educated colonized, reifying the colonial regime's claims to omnipresence, omnipotence and omniscience.

The story itself is Saratchandra's unconscious reflection and perhaps a regurgitation of the colonial state's imperialistic discourse on the establishment of the rule of law in a disorderly and chaotic land, where thugs and other criminal castes and classes carried out their mysterious rites and their nefarious and murderous activities with no let or hindrance.[14]

> Many have heard of the thugs (Thangarays) and those who are as old as I am, have also had the privilege of seeing them in real life...
>
> As a boy, I was really addicted to fishing...When I used to roam about on my own in search of...fish...I have...seen dead bodies covered in mud and slime... On both the river banks, there were heavily wooded forests, and who knew from where these dead men had come, or where they had been killed by these thugs...I have never seen the police come...nor have I seen anybody from the village go and put in a complaint...[15]

The young narrator recounts the story of his misadventure with these thugs. Factors concomitant to the concept of caste—hierarchies, effortless domination and unquestioning submission—foreground the story's unfolding. The young

---

[14]William Henry Sleeman, *A Journey, Through the Kingdom of Oude in 1848-1850,* Vol. 1, London: Richard Bentley, 1852. See also Radhika Singha, *A Despotism of Law: Crime and Justice in Early Colonial India,* Delhi: Oxford University Press, 1998.

[15]'A Day's Tale', in *SSS,* Vol. 2, p. 1771.

Brahmin boy (who remains unnamed throughout the story), despite his grandmother's flat veto, runs off in the wake of Nayan Baagdi, an erstwhile low-caste thug, but now turned into a devout Vaishnav. Nayan owed his release from the colonial legal system due to the grandmother's legal help. He was now her most devoted servant. He had come to take five rupees from the grandmother for the purchase of a cow in a distant village, while the young boy was wishful of getting fishing rods. On the return journey with the cow, they see a poor Vaishnav mendicant get murdered, and the story then unfolded new complexities.

Nayan Baagdi is at first horrified, and then enraged. His old life, buried under a Vaishnav's robe, reasserts its existence, and he resolves to avenge this murder. But even in the middle of contemplating extreme violence, he shouts to the murderers lurking behind the trees, according to the child narrator:

> Nayan-da suddenly stopped dead and yelled—what a terrible voice that was—'*Khabardar*, I say to you all! There is a Brahmin boy with me. You dare throw the *pabada* at us and I will not leave a single man alive, and so I am warning you!'[16]

The Brahmin boy, as the narrator, first evinces real terror, but the instant he realizes he is on the winning side, he immediately and jubilantly appropriates his protector/companion's identity of an invincible dacoit for himself[17]:

---

[16]'A Day's Tale', in *SSS*, Vol. 2, p. 1773.

[17]To be a dacoit and lawbreaker was/is a fantasy for many children. See Mark Twain, *Tom Sawyer & Huckleberry Finn*, Wordsworth Classics, Hertfordshire, Rep. 1992, pp. 71–93.

I began to jump on the spot at the good news. I called out to him, 'Catch him and bring him here, I will beat him to death. Don't you kill him.'

'No, dada, you will do the killing.'[18]

However, faced with the reality of the action, and the fully transformed face of the guard he had taken to be a tame servant, the child dimly realizes that Nayan and he belong to separate worlds.

Nayan-da's voice had changed completely, his face belonged to someone else. His transformed appearance smote me with a chill of fear. Instead of starting a new game, my hands and feet began to shake uncontrollably, and I said tearfully, 'I cannot, Nayan-da.'

The boy then proposes to hand him over to the police, an action that is comfortingly rooted in his middle-class ethics and textbooks.

At this, suddenly Nayan-da started and said, 'In the thana? In the hands of the police?'

'Yes. He has killed a man, and so they should hang him. As you sow, so shall you reap.'

Nayan was quiet for a while; then he prodded the man with his lathi, and said, 'Hey, get up!'

But there was no response. Nayan said, 'Has the fellow died or what? The weakling—for two days perhaps he has not even had a fistful of rice—and he has hit the road to beat people to death! Go fellow, get lost! Get up and go home!' But the man remained inert. Nayan

---

[18]'A Day's Tale', p. 1774.

then bent down, held his hand near his nose, and said, 'No he is not dead. He is just unconscious. When he comes to, he will go home by himself. Come dada, let us also go home. It is now very late, your grandmother will be so worried.'[19]

The boy's dissatisfaction with this departure from the stringent punishment specified in textbooks, is clear. However, Nayan clearly feels that to kill a murderer might be defensible, but to surrender a man to the police would be betrayal. Chasms lie between the two worlds of the servant and the young boy. Saratchandra's refusal to take sides in this moral dilemma is real, but his narration from the upper-caste standpoint, especially the tacit approval he accords Nayan's reverential treatment of the grandmother, does not only betray Saratchandra's own social upper-caste rootedness, but also the entire social structure's. Meenakshi Mukherjee pertinently observes in another context: 'It is possible that Saratchandra did not make this concession consciously—his inhibitions might have happened to coincide with those of his readers....[20] Citing author Saroj Bandopadhyay, Mukherjee writes: 'There is far more complexity and contradiction in Saratchandra's handling of social hierarchy than in his treatment of women.'[21] Nayan Baagdi, can change in a flash from a loyal human watchdog, with a complete reverence for an upper-caste boy, into a dacoit. However, even as a dacoit, he retains his instinctive respect for social hierarchies. Ranajit Guha's re-reading of Dinabandhu Mitra's *Neel Darpan*, had similarly demonstrated

---

[19]'A Day's Tale', p. 1774.
[20]Mukherjee, *Realism and Reality,* p. 105.
[21]Ibid., p. 106.

that Mitra's 'revolutionary' and militant Torap was actually a construction of the middle-class intellectual. Middle classes projected their own requirements, desires and fantasies—about social power, authority and the natural obedience of the ideal servant, whose machismo would serve the interest of the upper classes and castes. Their hegemonic understanding of power was reflected—as Althusser had so compellingly shown—in the production of literature.

Saratchandra's unconscious production of precisely this power-equation, does not give the lie to his own statement of being the voice of the margins. It makes us aware of the web of power that produces social relations, which despite personal convictions running against them, somehow force their way into mental landscapes. Caste differentiations soak through even in the way Saratchandra maintains nomenclature in his stories, where upper-caste family names are always attached to honorifics—Chattujje-moshai/mohashoyey, and Mukhujje-moshai/mohashoyey. In direct opposition, for the lower castes, the caste category becomes the surname—Nayan Baagdi, Kaangaali Duley. It is perhaps highly significant that Saratchandra himself does not see the incongruity of valourizing Nayan's deification of the Brahmin widow, and that too in a story written for the edification of *children*.

Nayan would come and stretch out in obeisance to my grandmother whenever he felt like it. As he had no right to touch a Brahmin's widow, he would pluck a leaf from a tree and place it near her feet, she would touch it with her big toe, and then he would place the leaf reverently on his forehead and neck, and say, 'Didithakrun, bless me so that I am reborn in an honest caste, that I can take the dust from your feet with my hands.' Thakurma would say lovingly, 'Nayan, I bless you so that you are reborn as a Brahmin.'[22]

The story shows two moral worlds: one heavily influenced by the colonial experience, and another that is shaped by the new expectations from a middle-class perception of an all-powerful state. One needs to remember that the Saratchandra who fulminated against British rule as a Congress worker, who talked about sacrifices for the motherland, is also (that too to children) talking about the stamping out of Thuggi in '50–60' years of British rule! It shows that the discourse of law and order the colonial state had leaned on heavily as its claim to legitimacy had borne fruit: so much so that a popular writer and a representative of the average middle-class Indian nationalist, duplicated the colonial state's logic.

Nayan's world is vaguely perceived as dark, obscure, mysterious—definitely violent. The tip of the iceberg—or the socially accepted Nayan—is pious, obedient, reverential, even transformed by the acquired middle-class trait of literacy. But Nayan can kill for revenge, and the reassertion of his old identity as a thug terrifies the boy who looks upon him as an inferior. Further, Nayan cannot betray a man who comes from his world to the colonial state—something that the boy has learnt to do effortlessly—i.e., pass the buck of punishment to the colonial state. With all his inhibitions, Saratchandra does perceive that though these two worlds interlock, spatially, they are located separately.

'The Child-snatchers' (Chheley-dhora), as a story, also

---

[22]'A Day's Tale', *SSS*, p. 1773.

emanates from a similar, dark, uncolonized world, where suspicion, fear and superstition obfuscate the mind, and make violence and brutality the inevitable expressions of such mindscapes. Infanticide and child sacrifice sprang out of an untamed, indigenous imagination. Even the colonial state's development projects were given a dark indigenous colouring, like the construction of a bridge over the local river needed a religious safeguard: the colonial state's minions had been directed to bury three children alive for the successful operationalization of the bridge. The villagers were convinced that the colonial state had secretly employed child-snatchers to ensure the unhindered progress of their plans. The story, against this background of suspicion about the colonial state in a village-community, narrates the reluctance of an elderly and childless couple, the Mukhujjes (Mukhopadhyays), to surrender half of the ancestral property (utensils and the like) to their nephew. The nephew hires two local Muslim roughs to scare his Khudo and Khudi (uncle and aunt) to give him his rightful share. The story turns on the comic effect produced when the plan backfires. The villagers lynch the two strangers as 'child-snatchers'. Here too, the 'ordinary', like Nayan's world, can be outside the control of the colonial state, a zone where fears, superstitions and murders are phantasmagorical, yet a part of the living reality. The narrator, a middle-class voice of rationality and a face of a responsible citizen, provides the new 'humane' logic of the colonial state:

> Just at that moment, I happened to be passing that way, and hearing the disturbance, I came down to the pond to investigate. When they saw me, the excited crowd once again erupted into a loud speech. They all shouted

in unison that they had caught a child-snatcher. When I looked at the man, his condition brought tears to my eyes, he did not even have the strength to speak; his face was a big mess of sideburns, sindoor, turban and blood. He could only weep and fold his hands.

I asked, 'Whose child has he stolen? Who has complained about him?' They said, 'Who knows?'

'Where is the child?'

'How should we know that?'

'Then why are you flogging him like this?'

Someone intelligent said, 'He must have buried the child in the mud. He will dig the child out at night. He will then sacrifice him and bury him in the pool.'

I said, 'How can a dead child be sacrificed?'

They said, 'Why should it be dead? The child will be alive.'

'If a child is buried in the mud, can it remain alive?'

To many, this logic sounded convincing. Nobody till then, under the grip of all the wild excitement, had been inclined to think along these lines.[23]

It is evident from the above passage that while the single educated voice is rational and reacts humanely to human distress, the collective voices of the uneducated are irrational, their actions frenzied, cruel and illogical; they are the 'uncolonized indigenes'. They are incapable of reason and are under the sway of their own myths, fears and practices.

The three *Laalu* stories, while light-hearted, are again grounded in the social fabric of village life. Laalu, figuring in

---

[23]'The Child-snatchers', in *SSS*, Vol. 2, pp. 1768–69.

all the three stories, is a rebel, though much admired within the village. However, in these three stories, as well as in 'Ekadashi Bairagi', 'Bilasi', and 'Childhood Memories' (Balyo-Smriti), one sees minors (specifically boys) as active members of the community: for rendering services during festive seasons, for cremating the dead, for providing aid, or in beating up recalcitrant/immoral fellow villagers. Laalu is an understudy of Indranath, the latter supposedly modelled on Saratchandra's friend Rajivkumar Majumdar, from their childhood days in Bhagalpur. Laalu, like Indranath, could not be considered an ideal role model for the average, educated Bengali boy.

In *Laalu*, the more socially reprehensible traits like smoking pot and bidis have been expunged, but the refusal to be rule-bound, or be tied down to ordinary middle-class aspirations, persist. Saratchandra, possibly thinking back on his own childhood, feels that childhood and youth should not be too fixated on the eventuality of adulthood, or be bent on acquiring the right kind of training to achieve the maximum material advancement as a 'successful' adult. This glorification of an impulsive and heedless childhood, a living in the present, a lack of fear with regard to the future, is a constant haunting refrain of Saratchandra. At its strongest in the first three episodes of Srikanta's adventures with Indranath, it is fairly loud in 'Bilasi' (1917 [1324 BS]), 'Childhood Memories' and the Laalu stories written between 1935–37. As this is a fairly constant theme across a long temporal stretch, lasting right up to Saratchandra's last set of publications for children, and one that kept surfacing as a call to 'passion' and 'selflessness' in the author's exhortations to the youth of Bengal, one can perhaps conclude that Saratchandra defined childhood and youth as periods where ideals, idealism and a passionate and active commitment to these ideals existed. They were not to be times when one had to be careful, calculating, and ambitious in the worldly sense. Saratchandra thus, constantly turned to the 'youth' of Bengal with this mental template in place, hailing its spirit as the deliverers of colonized India.

Thus, while the first 'Laalu' fondly remembered a prankster, the second had moved on to the story of a youngster who refused to travel on the same road as his peers. He had bid goodbye to further education, and struck out on his own as a young labour contractor. Perhaps the class-angle had escaped Saratchandra in his celebration of an individualistic and self-willed youngster who had the strength of mind to repudiate the standard middle-class educational grind for professional advancement. There are shadowy figures, like Laalu's father, who had achieved material success and arduously climbed social ladders through this hard but tried-and-proven method (treading after the ghost of Vidyasagar). In the third Laalu story, the daredevil makes a spectacular reappearance. As a youngster who thought nothing of being alone in a crematorium at night, with a dead person struck down with cholera, it celebrates the spirit of fearless 'boyhood', far removed from the sheltered world of young girls and the oppressive world of the underprivileged.

Saratchandra maps two different kinds of middle-class male children. The child narrator of 'A Day's Tale From Some Fifty Years Ago', who does not feel uneasy at social gulfs between human beings, who is bookish and is already weighing up ethical positions from the safe haven of textbooks, is clearly travelling the well-trodden path of future middle-class professional achievement. There is no 'rebel' hiding in this story and he already knows how to tell a hair-raising tale to his grandmother which will suitably terrify her, but without mentioning his own fears:

> ...the moment I put a foot inside the house, I burst into speech with suitable gesticulations of all my limbs, and poured forth the story of our victory over the thangarays and all the stirring events that had followed our purchase of a cow, of course omitting such irrelevant details like trembling hands and legs. Grandmother listened to me with great attention, and then she heaved a sigh and held me close without saying a word.[24]

This young narrator, though treated with sympathy and humour, and in an autobiographical vein, is indeed in sharp contrast to Saratchandra's more 'masculine' protagonists.

'Childhood Memories', published with the last set of stories in *Chhelebaelar Golpo*, brought out posthumously in 1938, slips behind the tough exterior of the non-conformist rebel to unravel his inner complexities. Unmanageable, self-willed, a tobacco-smoker and a school dropout, Sukumar claims to mock his name, for the name signifies a '"good" boy'. He cares nothing for harsh whippings, or for the remonstrations of his elders. But, when he is transplanted from the village to Calcutta for pursuing his education, he copes quite well with the challenges of a classroom. He would have perhaps been moulded like everyone else, but for his friendship with the Brahmin cook, Gadadhar, a powerless servitor. This friendship allows him to develop a perception of inequalities, of oppression and of scarcity. He realizes that his actions expose the vulnerable Gadadhar Brahmin to false accusations, unjust

---

[24]'A Day's Tale', p. 1775.

pecuniary penalties and finally an outright dismissal from the job as a thief. He develops a conscience, and a certain insight into the immunity his own social status gives him. The story is a strange mix of a regretful confession of a young boy's lack of moral fibre to take the rap for his own misdeeds, and his deep shame at the blame constantly being laid at his friend's door, because he is a servant, hapless and voiceless.

III

The story also links the middle-class world to the invisible worlds the underprivileged groups occupied at the time. The second set of stories turns around the underprivileged communities and social groups. Though Saratchandra did not claim to represent more than the human abject, two stories in this collection also look very closely at a bullock (in 'Mohesh') and a dog (in 'Memories of Deoghar'/Deogharer Smriti), a treatment which forces us to ask whether the anthropomorphic frame is the only one window available to us for examining our relation to the world.

As Swapna Banerjee points out in her work on *Men, Women and Domestics*,[25] servants were not necessarily from the lower castes. Personal comforts and respectability were achieved owing to the presence of their labour, but it was socially necessary to mark them out as the 'Other', to turn them into either obedient and loyal servants, or push them into slippery zones of duplicity and untrustworthiness. Saratchandra's 'Childhood Memories' does both. Sukumar might have an affective bond with Gadadhar, he might feel secretly responsible that Gadadhar

---

[25]Swapna Banerjee, *Men, Women and Domestics: Articulating Middle-class Identity in Colonial Bengal*, Delhi: Oxford University Press, 2004.

constantly ran into foul weather with his employer, Sukumar's cousin, but he also does not hesitate to thrash another servant with leather sandals, and then recommend the make to the reader—for despite such hard use, the sandals remain intact.

There were legal provisos in the Indian Penal Code against assault and battery, but these did not hold any meaning for the bhadralok where a servant's bodily boundaries were concerned. A servant, however close a bond he may have shared with the brother of his employer, would not breach certain limits—Gadadhar always addresses Sukumar as 'Chhotobabu'. Saratchandra perhaps used Sukumar as a lens for examining the helplessness of servants. The servant always occupied a liminal position where his trustworthiness was undecipherable. This trust had to be renewed on an everyday basis, and the finger of suspicion always remained alert, waiting to be raised. A middle-class interlocutor questioned this readiness to condemn and maltreat a particular servant—without arriving at a larger ethical conclusion about the injustice of such an action. It is an incomplete realization, but Saratchandra seems to suggest, that even a partial vision of such oppressive social attitudes elided most employers.

A similar concern is expressed for a ten-to-twelve-year-old Kayastha[26] boy forced to work as a servant in the eponymous story 'Haricharan'. The boy was an indefatigable worker, blessed with good looks, and an unquenchable smile, which had won for him the goodwill of both the master and the mistress of the household. Saratchandra uses these voices to underline the fact that the boy worked hard, willingly, and so deserved love, and the epithet 'poor little orphan'. The twenty-year-

---

[26]Caste of scribes

old son of the family, upon his return to his ancestral home, adopts the boy as his personal servant as he is 'intelligent'. Saratchandra ironically uses the word 'love' to describe the young man's feelings for Haricharan. The little boy helps the young man bathe, prepare his hubble-bubble, press his feet, make his bed. However, despite such willingness to wait on the young man hand and foot, Haricharan is unable to escape kicks and a whipping, when because of fever he falls asleep and has left the bed unmade, the hubble-bubble unprepared, and was obviously not waiting to press the young man's feet when he returned home at two in the morning. While the climax of the story—a small postscript at the end of the letter mentioning Haricharan's death—is unnecessarily charged with sentimentality, Saratchandra quite effectively shows the indifference of a certain social strata to the service classes. He seems to sardonically note that there may even be some recognition of shame or regret, but such feelings are fleeting and shallow.

'Bilasi', written at the request of Rabindranath Tagore in 1917,[27] is a critical assessment of a village community. The eponymous low-caste female protagonist in 'Bilasi' is seen through the reflexive gaze of a 'respectable' young man, Nyadaa.[28] Nyadaa's adult eyes constantly flicker to a childhood spent in the village and dwells particularly on an ineffective and stupid youth, Mrityunjoy, a Kayastha by caste and an orphan who could not move beyond the third class (class VIII). His uncle only coveted Mrityunjoy's orchard. A local snake charmer

---

[27]In 1324 (BS), at Tagore's request again, it was presented at a gathering of *Bichitra*.

[28]Nyadaa was also Saratchandra's own nickname.

and his daughter Bilasi from the unclean locale of Malpaḍa, epitomizing human kindness, manage to pull Mrityunjoy through a fatal illness. This leads to an inter-caste marriage, and the village rallies round to the side of moral rectitude. The village stalwarts, Nyadaa included, condemn the sin of a Kayastha eating rice out of the hands of a low-caste female, lock up the still bedridden Mritunjyoy, thrash the girl, drag her out of the village by her hair, and purge the village of pollution. Consequently, the couple become residents of Malpaḍa.

Nyadaa, doubtful of this brand of moral policing and ashamed of his own role in it, seeks refuge in pursuing a sannyas, but is forced to return to the village because of the mosquitoes in the wild. He encounters the young couple—both of whom are by then snake charmers—and is immediately attracted to such an 'adventurous' lifestyle. Bilasi is far more knowledgeable about snakes and their habits than the two young men, but the young adventure-seeker does not pay any heed to her warnings, as a result of which Mritunjyoy dies of snakebite. Bilasi stays alive long enough to extract a promise from Nyadaa that he will give up such dangerous entertainment, and eventually commits suicide. The narrator, including himself in such a narrow and self-seeking social structure, reveals a blinded and crippled social world, where no one can see beyond the norms of caste and self-interest. The village then turns into a micro-study of the darkness of self-inflicted misfortunes of an entire rural community, except that the victims remain unaware of their social and mental barrenness.

The two stories, 'Mohesh', after the eponymous bull, and 'Abhaagi's Heaven' (Abhaagir Swarga), reveal similar micro-studies of blinded village communities, at best indifferent to human misery, at worst, complicit in enforcing oppressive social norms and customs, and condemning the marginalized social groups to a subhuman existence.

Mohesh, the beloved old bull of Gofur, past his prime, but precious beyond mere utility, is a mere religious symbol for a Brahmin-dominated Hindu village. There is no affect in this mechanical revering of a religious symbol. All the life-sustaining elements—grass in the village commons, water in the ponds— are relentlessly controlled by the powerful Hindu social groups. The helpless Muslim peasant and his long-suffering ten-year-old daughter try to control a famished bull (who occasionally goes on the rampage for fodder and water), pay taxes and cope with droughts. Gofur, goaded beyond endurance at a public beating because of Mohesh's trespassing the zamindar's garden, and for breaking his daughter's precious earthenware vessel full of water, because Mohesh wanted to quench his thirst—kills the bull. The oppression from the Hindu zamindar because of this killing and his own heartbreak over Mohesh's death, finally drive Gofur and his daughter Amina out from his bit of land in the village.

In 'Abhaagi's Heaven', Abhaagi, belongs to the Duley community and bearing a name meaning the 'unfortunate', given to her by her father, lives up to her name. Her little son Kaangaali (the 'homeless') and she had been abandoned by the husband, and Abhaagi had to struggle to make a living for herself and Kaangaali for fifteen years. However, just when Kaangaali is learning a trade, and an end to this struggle for survival seemed at hand, Abhaagi falls in love with Death, seen from afar as the funeral procession of a Brahmin mistress of a well-to-do household. Death appears as beautiful, plenteous, desirable and full of promise as the ultimate release at the hands of a son—the hands of a son carrying fire. The elderly Brahmin husband as a calm-faced mourner, giving his departing lifelong companion dust from his feet, is also a part of this grand exit from the world. The Divine chariot is clearly carrying the fortunate woman, red sindoor in the parting of her hair, red lacquered feet put up in rest.

Abhaagi feels she can also manage this wonderful exit, for she too has a son, and a husband. It only requires that the son provide the fire and the husband bestow on her the dust from his feet—and she too would achieve this splendid exit from a miserable life to everlasting joy in heaven. Abhaagi then wills herself to die of fever though she is not quite thirty; but life seems dull in contrast to a 'sati's' death. The husband, moved to tears by such a request from a discarded but still a 'sati' wife, provides the dust from his feet, and so fulfils the first criteria of Abhaagi's dying wish for this could be managed without fees and taxes. But the dead woman's desire of fire at the hands of her son meant burning wood on a funeral pyre. And this—even though the tree in question had been planted by Abhaagi herself—required permission from the zamindar to be cut down. In two hours, Kaangaali grows old, trying to get permission from the authorities for cutting down the tree his mother had planted. He gets no wood from the whole village, and finally has to listen to a Brahmin's sage advice—accordingly he begins the process of burning the body by placing the bundle of straw, its end alight with fire, to his mother's lips, and buries her body on the bank of the local river.

Both Amina, Gofur's daughter, and Kaangaali, a Duley's son, are adults while still children. Saratchandra's four-page long stories show this quick transition. From childhood as ideology to childhood as a quick step to adulthood—in short to a life as lived by the parents—show the differences of class and life opportunities starkly. The life of the girl child is particularly clearly drawn: whatever might be the life of a girl in a higher economic and social bracket, Amina can certainly claim no leisure: nowhere in the story, for instance, is she shown playing. On the contrary, she is much older than her years, and comprehends not only preparing a meal with hardly any available ingredients, but also the principle of non-wastage. She is a Muslim girl, and her daily struggles at the village well with a pot waiting for her turn is also not the mere imagination of the author. While 'Mohesh' and 'Abhaagi's Heaven' are not read to connect different experiences of childhood as lived by different castes/communities/social classes, these stories can also be read as experiences of growing up in contexts ridden with enormous social, political and economic disadvantages.

The last story, 'Ekadashi Bairagi', is indicative of Saratchandra's optimism. While the village community is still oppressive, blind, self-serving, cruel and opportunistic, change is inevitable and it is the middle-class youth who will generate a different way of looking at things. Thus, Apurba, a Brahmin youth, remains apparently grounded in his customary village power hierarchies even with an education in Calcutta. However, he is intelligent, and has developed a certain urban sociopolitical breadth of vision in the political and social ferment of Calcutta.

Saratchandra, as a contemporary commentator on the excesses of a Hindu religious identity, mocks the credulousness of school and college lads at swallowing hook, line, and sinker the 'modern scientific rationale' to justify all customary practices in the 'sanatana' Hindu dharma. He frames Apurba's zeal in his justification of the 'tuft', for it aids the conduction of electricity through the body, or the benefits from Brahminic rituals, as fads. The nation-state seen through these lenses was bound to appear distorted, as Saratchandra ironically observes: 'The entire youth population were galvanized into programmes for the complete rejuvenation of the Hindu dharma as well as the nation.'[29]

Thus, the lad's enthusiasm, bounded by religious and social identities, is at first limited to narrow goals, and Apurba is not above using the punitive social customs of the village for certain 'sociocultural' gains. He is thus willing to compel Ekadashi Bairagi, the local moneylender, whose beloved sister has a social black mark against her name, to disgorge a huge sum of money for the rejuvenation of the school library in the village. However, at the end of the story, he realizes that the social outcasts are much superior to his 'pure' Brahmin friends, and suddenly the hollowness of caste practices bursts in on him. Saratchandra feels optimistically that youth will be the conduits of change, a conviction which is also reflected in his political essays and his exhortations to the youth of Bengal.

As in 'Mohesh', where the bull is sketched in with amazing feeling, so also the last story, written towards the end of Saratchandra's life, when he had gone for a change of air to Deoghar, and had dedicated a short essay to the memory of a street dog who had borne him company in his two and a half

---

[29]'Ekadashi Bairagi', in SSS, Vol. 1, pp. 779–84. In the late nineteenth and twentieth centuries, Hindu Dharma Sabhas became very active and held public lectures about Hinduism as a scientific and modern religion, despite its antiquity. There were modern, scientific (read Western science) reasons for all Brahminic rituals and customs, proving to the 'modern' Hindu that whatever the Western sciences advanced as 'new' knowledge, had been known to the 'ancient Hindus'. Shashadhar Tarkachuramani was a Hindu proponent of such ideas.

months of stay there, also stand in for a metaphor of human betrayal and animal devotion. In *The Open*, Giorgio Agamben diagnoses the history of both science and philosophy as part of what he calls the 'anthropological machine' through which the human is created with and against the animal.[30] Who is included in human society and who is not is a consequence of the politics of 'humanity'. We find that Saratchandra is conscious that this man/animal divide is a 'production' of precisely such an 'anthropological machine'—a divide not just applicable to the animals but also lethal for certain kinds of human beings.

Saratchandra is still relevant as a writer for his outrage that this 'anthropological machine', inscribing differences between the human and the animal, and more disturbingly, between the human and the not-human, which helps in normalizing violence, while erasing mental discomforts about it. However, he also is a voice from the colonial past, which reminds us of a horizon of expectation that could not project thinking, politically self-conscious, politically active, underprivileged communities and classes. As we read his concerns, he turns into our contemporary, and as we critically look at his limits, he shrinks into a distant historical frame, demonstrating to us that the past leaps into the present and can be projected into the future, through our own acts of reading.

---

[30]Georgio Agamben, *The Open: Man and Animal*, ed. Werner Hamacher and trans. Kevin Attell, Stanford: Stanford University Press, 2004.

section one

one

LAALU—ONE[*]

I had a friend when I was a boy—his name was Laalu. Half a century ago—in fact, so long ago that you cannot quite grasp the length of time that has passed by—we used to study together in the same class in a small Bengali school. We were then ten to eleven years old. There was no limit to the number of strategies that could come up in Laalu's head to frighten or harass others. Once, to frighten his mother, he had used a rubber snake to such effect that she twisted her ankle and had to limp around for a good seven days. Thoroughly annoyed, she said that a private tutor needed to be appointed for him. He will come in the evenings to make him sit to study, and Laalu would then not have the time to get up to his tricks.

But, Laalu's father said 'no' when he heard of this. He himself had never had any private tutors, had borne huge hardships in order to acquire a good education, and was now a successful lawyer. He desired that his own son be educated in a similar fashion. However, he stipulated that if Laalu failed to

---

[*]Translated from the original with the same title, in *SSS*, Vol. 2, pp. 1765–69.

top in his class at any time, a private tutor would be engaged for teaching him at home. Laalu managed to escape the big danger this time round, but he secretly nourished a grudge against his mother for it was she who was keen to saddle him with a tutor. In his opinion, to bring a private tutor into the home was just the same as bringing in the police.

Laalu's father was a wealthy householder. It had been a few years since the old homestead had been pulled down, and a new three-storeyed house had been built in its place. It had been the ardent wish of Laalu's mother ever since to invite her *gurudev*[1] to the new house, pay her obeisance to him and also seek his blessings. Unfortunately, he was old and generally reluctant to come so far out, all the way from Faridpur. But finally, she was granted the opportunity of serving her gurudev. Smritiratna had travelled to Kashi for ritually observing a solar eclipse, and he wrote to Nandarani that on his way back, he would bestow his blessings on her. Laalu's mother could scarcely control her joy—and instantly became completely absorbed in all the arrangements that had to be made for the visit. Her wish was about to come true—the dust from her gurudev's feet would purify her home.

All the furniture from the big room on the ground floor was removed: a new cot, made of light wood, arrived; new bedding arrived—gurudev needed a place to sleep. In a corner of the room, arrangements were made for his long hours of devotional rituals, as it would be difficult for him to go up and down the stairs to the *thakurghar*[2] on the third floor.

After a few days, gurudev arrived in person. But what a

---

[1]Spiritual preceptor
[2]Prayer room

tragedy! The weather turned foul; the entire sky was covered in dense black clouds and there was no let-up either in the constant downpour from the skies or in the storm.

Meanwhile, as all this was happening, Laalu's mother had no breath to spare: she was busy making sweets, arranging flowers and fruits, and in the middle of it all she also managed to make the bed, spread the sheets and tuck in the mosquito net with her own hands.

Conversations and the night rolled on, and it became quite late. The travel-weary gurudev had dinner, and finally sought his bed. The servants were dismissed. The soft and clean bed pleased gurudev no end, and in his heart, he showered blessings on Nandarani.

But suddenly, deep into the night, he awoke. Water, seeping through the ceiling, and through the mosquito net, was dropping onto his belly—Ooohhh! Wasn't it cold! He hurriedly got out of bed, wiped his stomach, and said, 'Nandarani, you may have constructed a new house, but I see that the strong westerly sun has already caused the ceiling to crack.' As the cot was of light wood, it was easy enough to drag it with its mosquito net to another side of the room, and compose himself again for sleep. But not even half a minute had elapsed, he had barely closed his eyes, when again droplets of icy water fell on precisely the same spot on his stomach. Smritiratna got up again, again dragged the bed to another part of the room, and observed, 'Eek! The ceiling seems to have cracked from end to end.' Again he lay down, and again water dripped onto his stomach. Again he dragged the bed to another side, but the moment he lay down, there was the same dripping water. Once again he dragged the bed to another side, but the end result remained the same. Now he saw that even the bed had become wet; it was impossible to lie down on it. Smritiratna felt beleaguered. He was old—he felt nervous of stepping out of doors in a strange place, but it was clearly dangerous to remain inside. What if the ceiling suddenly collapsed on him! He opened the door and in great trepidation, stepped out into the verandah; there was a lantern burning there, not a soul in sight and it was pitch dark.

It was raining hard, and the storm was still raging. It was difficult even to stand in it. He had no idea where the servants were or where they slept. He shouted loudly, but received no answer. There was a bench in one corner, and the poor clients who came to see Laalu's father normally sat there. Gurudev willy-nilly seated himself. He felt in his heart his sense of self-respect take quite a beating, but there was no way out of it. The northerly gusts of wind brought sharp sprays of rain—the chill was enough to raise goosebumps on exposed skin. He wrapped the end of his dhoti around himself, raised his feet as high as possible, and made himself as comfortable as possible under the circumstances. His body was numb with all the various types of weariness he had experienced through the day, his thoughts were bitter, his eyelids were weighted with sleep, his stomach was troubled by the unaccustomed heavy meal—the causes for irritation seemed endless! Suddenly, in such a situation there came yet another unforeseen new threat. The big mosquitoes of these western regions began to whine next to his ears. His tired eyelids in the beginning refused to respond to this new danger, but his heart instantly became fraught with anxiety—who knew how many they were? Just a couple of minutes, and then gurudev's apprehensions turned to cold certainty—gurudev understood they were infinite. In the entire world there existed no hero who was brave enough to disregard such an army. Their stings carried equal doses of burning as well as itchy sensations. Smritiratna hurriedly left the spot, but they accompanied him. Inside the room, the danger came from dripping water, and outside, it came from the mosquitoes. Their attacks continued relentlessly, notwithstanding the fact that he was constantly flourishing the end of his dhoti and waving his hands and feet to ward them off. Smritiratna rushed from one side of the verandah to the other. Even in the cold, he broke out into a sweat. He felt like giving vent to his feelings by bursting into tears, but he managed to restrain himself from indulging in such infantile behaviour. In his imagination he saw Nandarani peacefully and blissfully asleep in a soft bed with a mosquito net hanging around it, all the members of the household, wherever they were, cozily asleep wrapped in supreme peace—only there was no rest for him or to his mad dashes to and fro across the verandah. From somewhere in the distance, a clock struck four in the morning, and he said wearily, 'Go on, you horrors, do your worst—I give up.' So saying, he curled up in a corner, covering his back as much as he could by leaning against the wall and gave himself up to bitter reflections. It was now crystal clear to him as to why his mind had always suffered from those misgivings whenever he had contemplated a journey to these parts. He told himself, 'If I am alive until morning, I shall not spend an extra minute in this rotten place. I will board whichever train comes in first, and escape to my own place.' Slowly, sleep—that panacea for all sorrows—engulfed him, wiping out the misfortunes he had endured all through the night; Smritiratna, nearly unconscious, finally fell asleep.

Now, Nandarani was up before it was fully dawn—she had to attend to her gurudev's comfortable sojourn at her home. Last evening, gurudev had only partaken of snacks—admittedly quite heavy—and her heart was low with the certainty that gurudev had not dined well. Through the day, therefore, she would spare no pains to make up for the previous evening's paucity.

She came downstairs, and saw that the door stood open. She felt a little embarrassed to see that gurudev had woken up before her. She peeped into the room to find that he was not there, but something had surely happened. The cot that had occupied the southern corner of the room was now in the northern corner, his canvas bag had left the window sill and was now sitting on the middle of the floor, all the little vessels needed for his devotional practices were scattered across the room—the reason for such utter confusion completely past her comprehension. She emerged from the room and hailed the servants for none of them were yet astir. But then, where could gurudev have gone? Suddenly, her eyes fell on—'What was that? In the half darkness, wasn't that something like a human being sitting against the corner wall?' She summoned all her courage to her aid, walked ahead and bending a little forward, identified her gurudev. In a sudden nameless dread, she cried out, 'Thakurmoshai! Thakurmoshai!'

Smritiratna, called forth from his slumbers, opened his eyes, and slowly straightened his body to an upright position. Nandarani, deeply worried, ashamed and fearful, burst into tears as she asked, 'Thakurmoshai, what are you doing here?'

Smritiratna stood up and said, 'There was no end to my sorrows last night, maa.'

'Why, baba?'[3]

---

[3]Here, 'baba', and in the previous line 'ma', aren't meant to connote 'father' and 'mother' respectively. They are forms of address demonstrating reverence and affection.

'Maa, you have constructed a new house, but the ceiling is completely cracked. It has not rained outside last night, but all over my body throughout the night. Wherever I dragged my bed, water dripped over it. Fearing that the ceiling would fall on me, I came outside, but even that was no protection—the whole night hordes of locust-like mosquitoes have sucked me dry—I have been running from this side to the other and back again. Maa, half my blood has been drained from my body.'

Nandarani's eyes filled with tears as she contemplated the sorry plight of her aged gurudev, whose long-anticipated presence in her home, after repeated pleas and requests, had been a source of such intense joy to her. She said, 'But baba, the house is three-storeyed, there are two more rooms above yours—how could the rain water seep down through three levels?' Even as she spoke, it occurred to her that it could be some devilish stratagem of that wicked boy, Laalu. She ran to the bed and her groping hands found the sheets soaked in the middle, while there were drops of water still running down the mosquito net. She quickly took down the net and found a still-melting piece of ice wrapped in a bit of cloth. She rushed out like a mad woman, and to the first servant who came into view, she loudly rapped out the command—'Where is that hellhound Lelo?[4] Forget about your duties—go grab him from wherever he is and bring him here—and mind you, give him a drubbing on the way!'

Laalu's father was coming down the stairs at that moment, and he was amazed at his wife's conduct, 'What has happened? What are you doing?'

Nandarani burst into tears and said, 'Either you chase your

---

[4] An abusive distortion of Laalu's name as his mother was in a furious temper.

Lelo from this house for ever, or I shall drown myself in the Ganges and atone for this great sin!'

'But what has he done?'

'Come and see with your own eyes what he has done to gurudev for no fault of his.' Everyone entered the room. Nandarani narrated all, showed all. Then she asked her husband, 'How am I to hold a household with such a wicked boy, you tell me?'

Gurudev had by now understood the whole matter. He burst out laughing at his own stupidity.

Laalu's father stood rooted to the spot, his gaze fixed in the opposite direction.

One of the servants came and reported, 'Laalu-babu is not at home.' Another came and reported that he was sitting in his aunt's house and eating. His aunt had not permitted him to leave.

'Aunt' meant Nanda's younger sister. Her husband was also a lawyer; they stayed in a different neighbourhood.

For the next fifteen days, Laalu did not set a foot on even the boundaries of their house.

two

LAALU—TWO[*]

*H*is pet name was Laalu. He must have had some proper name, but it has slipped out of my memory. You perhaps know that in Hindi, the term '*lal*' means 'favourite'. I have no idea as to who had given him this nickname, but seldom has there been such a congruence between a person and his name. He was indeed a great favourite with everybody.

After school, all of us joined college, but Laalu said he would pursue some independent business. He asked his mother for ten rupees and became a 'contractor' on the strength of that. We said, 'Well Laalu, your capital is ten rupees.' He laughed and retorted, 'How much more does one want? This is more than sufficient.'

Everybody was fond of him, he managed to get jobs. On our way to college, we would frequently spot Laalu, with an umbrella over his head, and a few labourers with him, engaged in small road repairs. He would grin seeing us, and tease, 'Run, run! You will score a duck in the attendance register.'

---

[*]Translated from the original with the same title, in *SSS*, Vol. 2, pp. 1769–71.

When we were younger, in a Bengali-medium school, he used to be the handyman for all of us. In his school rucksack, there were always waiting in readiness a head of a pestle, a *norun*[1], a broken knife, an old head of a harpoon for making holes, a horseshoe—no one knew from where he had acquired these, and there was nothing he could not accomplish with these odds and ends. He would mend umbrellas for the whole school, fix the frames of slates, instantly mend clothes that had gotten accidentally torn while playing—countless such tasks. He would never say 'no' to any job. And he used to handle these tasks with great deftness. Once, during Chhat[2], he bought a few paise worth of coloured paper and *shola*[3], made attractive toys with them, and taking a position on the banks of the Ganges, he managed to make two rupees and fifty paise by selling them. He then treated us to a big treat of nicely fried peanuts.

As the years went by, we all grew up. There was no one to equal Laalu in the gymnasium. He did not just have tremendous physical strength, but also an equivalent share of courage. I think he really was not acquainted with the sensation of fear. He was ever-ready to respond to any call for help; he would be the first to reach a person in trouble. However, he had a terrible weakness—he just could not control the desire to frighten anybody if he saw an opportunity to do so. Before this compulsive desire, everyone—old as well as young—was

---

[1] A long thin iron tool with a very sharp edge at one end for cutting nails.
[2] Chhat is a Hindu festival of Bengal, also celebrated across India, in the name of Surya, the god of energy. It is celebrated four days after Diwali.
[3] It is a kind of papier-mache made from a plant growing in the wetlands in around Calcutta. It is a dying art form, as real estate business is taking over all the wetlands around urban spaces.

completely equal. None of us could imagine how, in an instant, such amazing ideas to terrorize people would unfailingly occur to him! Let me narrate one or two stories. In the locality, Manohar Chatterjee was performing Kali puja in his residence. Late at night, the local blacksmith was absent, yet the auspicious moment for sacrificing before the Goddess was fleeing fast. People rushed to his residence to fetch him, only to discover that he was senseless with colic pain. When they relayed the news to the others upon returning, the rest sat holding their heads in despair—where was the solution? From where could another executioner be found at that hour? The Goddess's worship was going to be ruined! Suddenly someone said, 'Laalu can behead goats. He has done it so many times.' People rushed to his place; Laalu awoke, sat up in bed, and said, 'No'.

'What no! If the Goddess's worship is interrupted, a terrible catastrophe will befall us!'

Laalu said, 'Let it happen, then. I have done such things when I was a boy, but I no longer do so.'

The persons who had come to call him banged their heads against the wall in despair: only ten or fifteen minutes to go, and then, all would be over, all destroyed. The wrath of the Goddess would kill everybody. Laalu's father ordered him to go. He said, 'These gentle folk have no other alternative and so have come to you. It will be wrong if you do not go. You must go.' It was impossible for Laalu to disobey such a command.

Chattujje Mohashoyey[4] felt reassured the instant he clapped eyes on Laalu. There was hardly any time. Swiftly a goat was dedicated to the Goddess; and it was quickly garlanded with red

---

[4]'Chattujje' is a popular and sometimes an anglicized version of the Bengali surname Chattopadhyay/Chatterjee. Mohashoyey is an honorific to express respect (as will be used in other stories in this collection as well).

hibiscus, sindoor smeared on its forehead, and then put into the sacrificial stock. The helpless, gentle being's last appealing bleats were completely drowned by the entire household collectively roaring out 'Maa! Maa!'[5] Laalu's hand holding the *khaanra*[6] rose, and an instant later, slashed downwards; from the severed neck a fountain of blood spouted and reddened the dark earth in a wet gush. Laalu closed his eyes for a moment. Gradually, the terrific clanging of *knasar*[7], the beating of drums, fell silent. The other goat, which had been trembling a little distance away, now in its turn, had its forehead daubed with sindoor, a red garland swung round its neck: again—the sacrificial stock, again the terrified last appeal, again the collective roaring of many voices—'Maa! Maa!' Once again, Laalu's hand holding the blood-stained khaanra rose and, in the blink of an eye fell: the beast's headless body beat a few times on the earth in a final plaint to Somebody and then it stilled; blood from its severed neck further reddened the already-red earth.

The drummers went mad on the drums, the many shouts from the completely packed courtyard rent the air. On the adjoining verandah facing the courtyard, Manohar Chattujje sat on a carpet, absorbed in meditating on the name of his *Ishtadevata*[8]. Suddenly, Laalu let loose a tremendous yell. Abruptly all noises ceased—everyone was struck dumb with amazement: 'What was happening!' Laalu's pupils were distended, his eyes were bulging and revolving fast in their sockets—he shouted, 'Where are the other goats?'

---

[5] 'Maa' here refers to the Goddess Kali.
[6] A falchion-like large knife with an extremely sharp edge used to butcher the goat for sacrifice.
[7] Metal cymbals
[8] Family deity

Somebody from the household, stuttering with fear, managed to say, 'There are no more goats. We always sacrifice just two.'

Laalu swung around the blood-stained khaanra in his hand above his head a couple of times and yelled in a terribly harsh voice, 'No more goats? No way! I am mad with bloodlust—either give me a goat now, or else I shall sacrifice before the Goddess whoever I can lay my hands on! Maa, Maa! Victory to Kali!' On the very utterance, with a gigantic leap he was over the sacrificial stock, his khaanra whirling madly in his hand. What happened after that cannot be described in mundane words. In one accord, everyone raced for the main exit, terrified in case Laalu would catch hold of any of them. In that desperate race, there was such an enormous pushing, elbowing and jostling that it felt as if a *Daksha yagna*[9] was being held once again. Some had fallen down and were still trying to roll away, some were crawling away and had managed to get their heads stuck between people's legs, some had their necks held in vice-like armpits and were gasping for breath, somebody had been trying to escape over another person, and had fallen flat on his face in the thick of the crowd—but all these frantic efforts lasted for the space of a second. The next, the place was totally deserted.

Laalu shouted loudly, 'Where is Manohar Chattujje? Where is the priest?'

The thin priest, under cover of the frightful din, was already safely hidden behind the idol of the Goddess. The family guru, seated on a grass-mat and engaged in reading religious tracts on Chandi, had hurriedly risen in the face of

---

[9]In the Vedas and the Indian mythological traditions, this is a ritual consecration around a sacred fire famously undertaken by Daksha, son of Prajapati, and which was disrupted by Lord Shiva.

the fracas and taken refuge behind a stout pillar. However, Manohar, inconvenienced by his huge girth, had found it difficult to run around for a safe hiding place. Laalu went forward, and gripping one of Manohar's hands with his left hand, said, 'Come and put your neck in the stocks.'

On the one hand, Laalu's iron fist, on top of which in his right hand was the khaanra: Manohar Chattujje almost died in fright. He began to plead tearfully, 'Laalu! Baba! Please calm yourself and look at me—I am not a goat but a human being. I am like your uncle through kinship, baba. Your father is like my younger brother.'

'I don't want to know! I am now ruled by bloodlust—come, I will sacrifice you. It is Maa's command.'

Chattujje burst into a loud wail, 'No, baba, it is not Maa's command, it can never be her command—Maa is the Mother of the Universe.'

Laalu said, 'Mother of the Universe! What do you know of that? Will you sacrifice more goats after this? Will you call me to sever goats' heads again? Speak!'

Weeping, Chattujje declared, 'Never again, baba, never again! I am swearing thrice in front of Maa—from today there will be no sacrifices ever again in my house.'

'Is that true?'

'Indeed it is true, baba, indeed it is true. Never again. Please let go of my hand, baba, I need to go to the toilet.'

Laalu loosened his hold, and said, 'All right, I am letting you go. But where did the priest run to? Where is the family guru? Where is he?' So saying, he again leaped across the courtyard and approached the *thakurdalan*[10]. There arose two

---

[10]Sacred yard

wails of fear in two different keys—one from behind the idol of the Goddess and another from behind the pillar. The mingled sounds of a reedy voice with a thick one were at once so peculiar and so comic that Laalu could contain himself no longer. 'Ha-ha-ha!'—he laughed and flinging the khaanra down on the ground with a bang, he ran out of the house.

It was then absolutely clear to everyone that all the talk of being under the influence of bloodlust had been a pack of lies, his idea of a joke. Laalu had been wickedly teasing everybody and frightening them all out of their wits. Within five minutes, everyone who had run away had returned and reassembled in the courtyard. There were still much that had been left incomplete in the worship of the Goddess because of the interruption. Amid the general hubbub, Manohar Chattujje began to swear repeatedly before everybody, 'If I do not make his father take a shoe to that rogue and make him smart under fifty blows by tomorrow morning, my name is not Manohar Chattujje.'

But Laalu did not smart under any blows from a shoe. He fled before daybreak to a secret place no one knew about, and not a whiff of his whereabouts for a good seven to eight days came through. After about a week, he stole into Manohar Chattujje's house after dark, and begged his pardon after making obeisance, and managed to escape from his father's wrath. Still, be that as it may, because Chattujje had taken an oath before the Goddess, goat-sacrifice during Kali-worship did come to an end in Manohar Chattujje's house from that time onwards.

three

LAALU—THREE[*]

*I*n our town, winter had arrived. Suddenly, cholera visited us. In those days, people used to become witless with fear at the mere mention of *olauthan*.[1] If anyone even heard of a case of cholera in the vicinity, no one would stay in that neighbourhood. If one died, to find someone to cremate the body would be well nigh impossible. But even in those difficult times, there was one person who never had any objections to such emergency calls. He was called Gopal-*khudo*[2], and his mission in life was to cremate dead bodies. If anyone was terminally ill, he would visit the doctor daily for news of the patient. If he heard there was no hope, he would arrive a couple of hours in advance, a towel flung over his shoulders. Some of us were his disciples. He would visit us with a grave face, and deliver standing instructions—'Hey, remain watchful

[*]Translated from the original with the same title, in *SSS*, Vol. 2, pp. 1775–77.

[1]Bengali term for 'cholera'.

[2]This stands for 'uncle', specifically father's younger brother; not necessarily a blood relation.

tonight. Mind you answer when I call. You remember the saying in the *shastra*s, yes? "*Rajdwarey shamshaneyca*"?[3]

'Yes, indeed. Of course we remember. The moment we hear your summons, we will set out with our towels over our shoulders.'

'Good, good, that's the spirit. This is the most sacred task in the world.'

Laalu was also part of our group. If he did not undertake any contractual job away from our locality, he would never say 'no' to such service.

That evening Khudo came to us wearing a long face, and reported, 'It seems like Bishtu pandit's[4] family wasn't spared after all.'

All of us started. When in school, we had studied Bengali under Bishtu pandit, a poverty-stricken teacher. He possessed a sickly constitution, and was completely dependent on his wife. He had no one else in the world—I have never seen anyone as harmless and helpless as he.

Around eight o'clock that night, we carried out the pandit's wife on a rope-cot, complete with all the bedding, from within the room to the courtyard.[5] Panditmoshai[6] looked on with vacant eyes. Nothing in this world could compare to that look, and when one saw it, one never forgot it.

When we were hoisting the dead body on our shoulders, panditmoshai said very softly, 'If I do not come with you, who will administer the *mukhagni*?'[7]

---

[3] A sloka from the Hitopadesa, conveying that in the king's court and in the cremation ground, work done is always propitious.

[4] Scholar, teacher in Sanskrit.

[5] An indication of a close-knit village community.

[6] A way of addressing an old, respected pandit.

[7] The first application of fire to the lips of the dead, administered generally by the son, the husband, or the father.

Before anybody could say anything at all, Laalu quickly said, 'That will be my responsibility, panditmoshai. You are our guru, and so she stands in the relationship of a mother to us.' We all knew that it was physically impossible for him to walk down to the cremation grounds. Just getting to school—a mere five minutes away from his house—used to take him half an hour of panting effort to accomplish.

Panditmoshai was quiet for a little while, and then he requested, 'Before taking her away, won't you put some sindoor on her head, Laalu?'

'Of course I will, of course I will,' affirmed Laalu, and leaping into the room, he brought out the little box and poured all its contents on her head.

We called out 'Hari bol'[8] and bore out panditmoshai's wife from the house forever—panditmoshai stood speechlessly in the open doorway with his hand on the door frame.

The cremation grounds were very far off, almost 3 yojans[9] away, located on the banks of the Ganges. When we reached it and had put the corpse down, it was two o'clock at night. Laalu touched the cot and sat on the ground with his legs thrust out before him. Some, out of weariness, lay down wherever they liked. The moon was three days short from full moon (it was shukla-dwadoshi)[10], and its refulgence lit up the gleaming sands on the cremation ground—absolutely soulless—across a vast distance. From across the river, an icy northerly wind ruffled

---

[8]While taking the body to the cremation pyre, the chant 'Hari bol' is uttered in a particular tune on the way. Hari is another name for Lord Vishnu or Krishna. 'Hari bol' literally translates to 'say Hari', i.e., to take the name of Hari in the face of grief.

[9]One yojan is equivalent to five miles or eight kilometres.

[10]The twelfth day of the waxing phase of the moon.

up the water into waves, some of which came and broke almost under Laalu's feet. The wood for the pyre normally came from the town in a bullock cart, but no one knew when it would finally arrive. Half a *krosh*[11] away there was the locality of the Doms[12].

Suddenly, from across the Ganges, a sharp wind began to drive a rapidly gathering black cloud towards us. Gopal-khudo took one look and then sighed, 'This is not looking good—there might be rain. In this weather, if we get wet, there is no saving us.'

There was no shelter, not even a big tree. A little way off, there was a small settlement of gardeners, dimly seen through the mango orchard that belonged to the Thakurbaadi. But it was not possible to run so far.

Soon, the entire sky became overcast, the moonlight was hidden in darkness, and from the other bank there came the sound of rainfall—and the sound began to draw nearer. In advance, a few drops fell on everyone like sharp arrows, and before we could think of anything, it began to pour. Abandoning the corpse, we ran helter-skelter for our lives.

It stopped raining in an hour's time, and then we all returned. The clouds had cleared, and the moonlight beamed forth and turned the night into day. The bullock cart had arrived in the meantime with the wood, and the driver had unloaded all the ingredients necessary for the burning of the body, and was now preparing to leave. But there was not a single Dom in sight. Gopal-khudo accusingly declared, 'Those rascals are like that. They do not want to stir out in the cold.'

---

[11]One *krosh* is equivalent to two miles.
[12]The untouchable caste that handles the task of cremation.

Moni said, 'But why isn't Laalu back? He was saying he would do the mukhagni. He did not run back home out of fright, I hope?'

Khudo directed his ire in the direction of the missing Laalu, and complained, 'Such is that fellow! If you are so fearful, why did you touch the body before sitting down? I would never have left the body, even if thunderbolts were crashing around me.'

'What happens if one leaves the body?'

Khudo said darkly, 'What happens! So many things might happen. It is, after all, the cremation grounds.'

'You would not have been nervous if you were alone with a body on the cremation grounds?'

'Fear? I? I have helped cremate at least a thousand bodies, do you know that?'

At that, Moni was silenced, for indeed Khudo could boast of his fearlessness. There were a couple of spades lying around on the grounds. Khudo picked one of these up, and directed, 'I shall dig out the firing-pit, you lot hand down the wood.'

Khudo was digging the pit, and we were bringing the wood down, when Noru observed, 'Look, hasn't the body swollen to twice its size?'

Khudo did not look around while he responded to this, 'Of course it has—it has been soaked in the rain water.'

'But cotton will shrink in volume if it is soaked, why will it swell?'

Khudo was annoyed and snapped, 'You are too clever! Continue doing what you are doing!'

We had almost finished bringing down the wood.

Noru's eyes were constantly on the cot. Suddenly he exclaimed, 'Khudo, the body seemed to move!'

Khudo was through with digging the pit. Now he threw aside the spade and said, 'I have never encountered such a coward like you, Noru! Why do you even come for these activities? Go, bring the rest of the wood. I will set up the pyre. Silly fool!'

A couple of minutes ticked by. This time it was Moni who suddenly started and said fearfully, 'Khudo, indeed it does not look good. The body did seem to move.'

Now Khudo burst into uproarious laughter, 'You people are planning to scare me? A person who has burnt over a thousand corpses?'

Noru pointed, 'Look, it is moving again.'

Khudo taunted, 'Yes, it is moving, it will become a ghost and gobble you up'—these words were scarcely out of his mouth when the corpse, rolled up in its bedding, quilts and blankets, knelt up on the cot and in a terribly nasal twang, shrieked, '*Naa, naa, Noruke(n) naa, G(n)opalke(n) khaa(n)bo*.'[13]

'*Orey baba re*!'[14] We fled with all our strength. Before Gopal-khudo was the stacked pile of wood, and as he could not run away with us, he dived straight into the freezing cold Ganges just behind him. He stood there, submerged up to his chest in the icy water and began to yell, 'Oh baba! I am finished! A ghost is about to eat me! *Ram-Ram-Ram-Ram*.'[15]

In the meantime, the ghost had flung back the covers from its head and had begun to shout, '*Orey* Nirmal, orey Moni, Orey Noru! Don't run away. It is I, Laalu, come back, come back.'

---

[13] The line translates to 'No, no, not Noru, will eat Gopal.' (The voice speaks in a nasal tone as it is supposed to be of a ghost's.)

[14] 'Orey baba re' is an expression that expresses fear or astonishment, something that can be a close equivalent to 'Oh my god'.

[15] '*Ram Ram*' is an incantation to ward off all supernatural appearances.

Laalu's voice reached us. We were all extremely embarrassed at our own idiocy and returned sheepishly. Gopal-khudo climbed up the bank, shivering with cold. Laalu touched his feet and offered shyly, 'When it began raining, everyone ran away, but I could not leave the corpse; so I took cover under the quilt.'

Khudo said, 'You did very well, it was a very quick-witted reaction. Now go, rub yourself well with the mud from the river and take a bath. I have not seen such a wicked boy in all my life.'

But he forgave him in his heart. He knew that even he would have found it impossible to match such fearlessness. The dead of the night, lonely vigil in the cremation grounds, a dead body, the bedding of a cholera victim—Laalu had ignored all these unhesitatingly.

When the question of mukhagni came up, Khudo objected—'No, that is not possible. If his mother gets to hear of it, she won't set her eyes on my face again.'

The cremation was over. When we returned home after bathing in the Ganges, the sun was just beginning to rise.

four

THE CHILD-SNATCHERS[*]

Some time ago, a sudden rumour spread across our region that unless three children were sacrificed, the railway bridge over Roopnarayan[1] just could not be constructed. Two small boys had already been buried alive under one of the pillions, and only one more needed to be caught. The bridge would be built in no time at all if only one more child could be kidnapped. It was heard that the rail company had appointed several child-snatchers who were wandering at will through the cities and villages. Nobody knew how and when they would show up. Some were dressed like beggars, some like wandering mendicants, and yet others carried long staffs in their hands like ordinary robbers. These were vintage rumours, and had been circulating for quite some time, and hence the villagers were beside themselves with fear and suspicion. Perhaps this time it would be their turn and it might be

---

[*]Translated from the original 'Chheley-Dhora', in *SSS*, Vol. 2, pp. 1767–69
[1]A broad and turbulent distributary of the Ganges in the Gangetic delta.

one of their kids who would be kidnapped and buried alive under the bridge.

Peace fled from people's minds, the residents of all the houses were spooked out. On top of all this, the newspapers added their mite in their reportage. The people who used to work in Calcutta would come back and relay these stories—the other day a child-snatcher was caught in Boubaazaar; yesterday, in Kodoha, a man had been caught red-handed just when he was putting a child into his sack—news such as these. News of Calcutta's by-lanes, where many innocents needlessly suffered simply because ordinary folk were suspicious of strangers, reached us through various people. As these conditions became fairly general, suddenly an incident took place in our 'country' too—I will narrate that tale now.

At some distance from the road, within a garden, there lived the old Mukhujje[2] couple. They had no children, but were intensely attached to all things related to materialistic pursuits and all matters related to domestic affairs. They had separated from their nephew, but had not separated themselves from the things to which the nephew could lay rightful claim. That they might part with these, had never even entered their imagination. Sometimes, the nephew would demand a few utensils and a few bits of furniture. His Khudi[3] would scream the place down, gather a large crowd around the homestead, and then complain, 'Hiru had come to hit us.'

Hiru would retort, 'That's the right way to go. I will thrash

---

[2]Mukhujje is the dialect for the surname 'Mukhopadhyay', or its anglicized version, Mukherjee.

[3]'Khudi' translates to Aunt. Below, 'Khudo' is meant for 'Uncle' (contrary to its usage in 'Laalu—3'.)

you one day and extract all the things which are mine by right.'

Days went by.

One morning, their quarrel reached its highest peak. Hiru stood in the courtyard and said, 'This is the last time I am saying this Khudo, will you disgorge what is rightfully mine or not?'

Khudo replied, 'You don't have a thing.'

'Nothing?'

'No.'

'I will not rest until I have extracted them from your clutches.'

Khudi was working in the kitchen; now she emerged and said, 'In that case, go get your father.'

Hiru returned, 'My father is in heaven, he will be unable to come, I will go and get your fathers. When they do turn up, they will divide the property. One of them might still be alive—they will come and fix my share to the hair.'

After that, my pen had to excuse itself from committing to paper the language that was exchanged between the two sides.

Hiru, while departing, declared, 'I will force matters to a rightful conclusion by today—this is for your information. Be warned.'

His Khudi scoffed from the kitchen, 'Yes, you have heaps of power! Go and do whatever you like!'

Hiru came straight to Raipur. There were a few households of poor Muslims here. On the day of Muharram, when they took out their *tazia*s,[4] they would wield heavy lathis. These lathis were well-oiled, and their joints strengthened with brass inlays. From this particular circumstance, many were convinced

---

[4]Processions with the faithful holding a green cloth over holy symbols.

that they were amazing *lathial*s[5], unparalleled and unmatched in the region. There was nothing they could not do. They kept a low profile merely because of the police. Hiru said, 'Bada Miyan[6], here, take these two rupees as advance—for you and for your brother. When you have successfully finished my work, you will be richly rewarded.'

Latif Miyan took the proffered two rupees, smiled and asked, 'Babu, what do you want done?'

Hiru answered, 'In this region everyone knows about you two brothers. Don't we all know that your lathis have been behind all those zamindaris that the Biswases have managed to grab? If you make up your minds, there is nothing you cannot do!'

Bada Miyan winked but said, 'Shh! Shh! Babu, if the local thana's *darogah*[7] comes to hear of this, all our protection from trouble will disappear. They know full well that we two brothers have given them (the zamindars) the possession of the entire village of Virnagar. We have escaped this time round only because no one recognized us.'

Astonished, Hiru asked, 'No one recognized you?'

Latif said, 'How could they? We had these huge turbans on our heads, sideburns on our cheeks, red sindoor plastered across the entire forehead, six-foot-long lathis in our hands—the people were convinced that *yamadut*s[8] had descended straight from the Hindu *yamapuri*[9]. Recognize us! They ran away as

---

[5]Experts wielding long bamboo staffs or lathis were known as *lathial*s or henchmen.

[6]An honorific for senior Muslim males.

[7]Police officer

[8]Messengers of death.

[9]The place where, after death, souls go.

fast as they could in every which direction!'

Hiru caught hold of his hand and said urgently, 'Bada Miyan, brother, you have to repeat that performance once again. My Khudo still thinks of giving me a bit of my share, but my Khudi is such a she-devil, she will not let me touch even a small water-jug! Put on those turbans, sideburns, all that sindoor, just stand there in that courtyard with your lathis in your hands, and give your dacoit's yell—then I will get to see what's what! I shall finally be able to yank out all that is rightfully mine. Just before it gets dark—all right?'

Latif Miyan agreed. It was decided that both the brothers, Latif and Mamud, would put on all their finery and then pay the Khudo and Khudi a visit. Hiru would be just behind.

It was *ekadashi*.[10] After fasting for the whole day, Jagadamba had set out the food on the verandah. Mukhujje-moshai had just sat down to some snacks. Just a bit of milk and fruits. He was slightly rheumatic, and heavy meals did not suit his constitution after a whole day of fasting. He had just raised a stone bowl filled with a little coconut milk to his lips, when suddenly in marched the two brothers, Latif and Mamud. They were wearing all their fancy attire— huge turbans, massive sideburns, sindoor smeared all over the forehead. The stone bowl crashed to the floor from Mukhujje's suddenly nerveless hands—while Jagadamba shrieked, 'Ahoy, neighbours—wherever you are, come here, child-snatchers have entered our house!'

In the small field in front of the houses, little children played hopscotch every day on roughly drawn squares. They were playing today, as usual. They too took up the cry as

---

[10]*Ekadashi* is just four days from full moon and a day of ritual fasting.

they scattered in every direction, running as hard as they could—'Ahoy, child-snatchers have come! They are taking away many children!'

Hiru had come along to direct them to the right house. He was hiding just behind the door. Now he said in a low tone, 'What are you waiting for Miyan—run for it! You will be beyond anyone's help if the people from the neighbourhood catch hold of you!' On those words, he himself legged it.

Latif Miyan may not have heard much news from the town, but the rumours of the child-snatchers had certainly reached him. He understood instantly that if they were found in an unknown place, dressed up as they were with sindoor daubed on their faces, all the bones in their bodies would be broken in case they fell into the villagers' hands. Therefore, they also ran for it. But where could they run to? The place was unknown, the daylight was failing fast—and from every corner there came collectively raised voices yelling—'Catch them, catch them! Kill the fellows!' The younger brother ran off to heaven knew where, but the villagers caught up with the elder brother, Latif, and quickly ringed him round. He managed to crash through a thicket of thorny bushes for dear life, and jumped into a small pond nearby. The villagers gathered on the banks and began to hurl stones at him. The moment he attempted to raise his head, stones pounded it. He would then once again duck back into the water.

Latif Miyan was half dead with the amount of water he had perforce drunk and the thick hail of stones. The more he attempted to plead with folded hands that he was no child-snatcher or that he had not come to kidnap children, the more angry and suspicious the people became. Why those sideburns then? Why was he wearing the turban? Why was his forehead covered in sindoor? His turban had unravelled long since, his sideburns were hanging from his cheeks, the sindoor on his forehead had partially washed off, and was smeared all over his face. However, what chance did he have of explaining all this to the villagers when the villagers were in no mood to listen to him?

By then, some enthusiastic people had waded into the water, and had pulled Latif out of the pond—while throughout, with folded hands he tried to convince them he was Latif Miyan, his brother was Mamud Miyan and they were not child-snatchers.

Just at that moment, I happened to be passing that way, and hearing the disturbance, I came down to the pond to investigate. When they saw me, the excited crowd once again erupted into a loud speech. They all shouted in unison that they had caught a child-snatcher. When I looked at the man, his condition brought tears to my eyes; he did not even have the strength to speak, his face was a big mess of sideburns, sindoor, turban and blood. He could only weep and fold his hands.

I asked, 'Whose child has he stolen? Who has complained about him?' They said, 'Who knows?'

'Where is the child?'

'How should we know that?'

'Then why are you flogging him like this?'

Someone intelligent said, 'He must have buried the child in the mud. He will dig out child at night. He will then sacrifice him and bury him in the pool.'

I said, 'How can a dead child be sacrificed?'

They said, 'Why should it be dead? The child will be alive.'

'If a child is buried in the mud, can it remain alive?'

To many, this logic sounded convincing. Nobody till then,

under the grip of all the wild excitement, had been inclined to think along these lines.

I said, 'Let him go.' I then asked the man, 'Miyan, what is the true story?'

Now, the man, a little emboldened, narrated the full story. Nobody had much sympathy for the Mukhujje couple, and some were moved to even feel some compassion.

I said, 'Latif, go home, and don't get into such imbroglios ever again.'

He pulled his nose and ears, he swore by the name of Allah and promised, 'Babumoshai[11], never again will I consent to such a thing. But where has my brother gone?'

I said, 'Latif, think of your brother after you get home. It is enough for now that you are escaping with your life.'

Latif, limping badly, somehow went home.

There arose another disturbance in the neighbourhood of the Ghoshals in the dead of night. Their maidservant had entered the cowshed to give the cows their feed. When she attempted to pull out the hay, she found that somehow it would not budge; suddenly a terrible figure emerged from inside the heap and wrapped its arms round the maidservant's feet.

The more the maidservant screamed, 'Ahoy, where is everybody, a ghost is about to eat me up'—the more the ghost put its hands on her mouth and begged, 'Oh, maa, please save me! I am no ghost or spirit, I am a human being.'

The screams brought out the master of the house with all the servants—all carrying lights—onto the scene. Everyone in the village had heard of what had passed earlier. Therefore,

---

[11]Honorific for gentlemen

the younger brother's luck held, and he did not face the same fate as his brother; people easily believed his assertion that he was Mamud Miyan and also that he was not a ghost.

Ghoshal let him go. He merely confiscated his beautiful lathi and said, 'Chhota Miyan, I am keeping this so that you will keep in mind what has happened all your life. Now go home quietly after washing your face of all that colour.'

The grateful Mamud offered a hundred salaams to Ghoshal, and quietly slipped away. This event is not a bedtime story for children, it did indeed take place in our village.

five

A DAY'S TALE FROM
SOME FIFTY YEARS AGO[*]

*M*any have heard of the thugs (*thangaray*), and those who are
as old as I am, have also had the privilege of seeing them
in real life. Just fifty to sixty years ago, in West Bengal—meaning
in the districts of Hooghly, Bardhaman and other neighbouring
districts—the threat from them was intense. Even before that,
roughly during my grandmother's time, I have heard that almost
no road after dark was safe for travellers. These miscreants were
as greedy as they were cruel. They would hide in the bushes
adjoining the roads in groups, heavy lathis in their hands and
also with small heavy bamboo sticks that they called *pabada*s.
When a traveller walked past, they would throw the pabada at
his legs with deadly accuracy. When he fell flat on his face on
the road under the unexpected attack, the entire group would
rush out and finish him off with heavy blows from their lathis.
They were ruled by no considerations or distinctions about

---

[*]Translated from the original 'Bochhor Ponchaash Purber Ekta Diner
Kaahini', in *SSS*, Vol. 2, pp. 1771–75.

their victims. I have seen many people with my own eyes, who had subsequently been murdered by these thugs.

As a boy, I was really addicted to fishing. Of course, it was not a grand affair at all—I used to go after small fish like *punti, chela* and the like. Almost before it was dawn, I would arrive at the river with my fishing rod in hand. At the end of our village, there was a little river, so shallow, that the deepest point was waist-high, smothered in weeds and slime, and in between, wherever there were bits of clear water, these fish would play about. Catching these on my baited hook used to give me enormous joy. When I used to roam on my own in search of these fish on the banks of the river, I have many a times seen dead bodies covered in mud and slime. Occasionally, the water used to be red from the blood that had flowed from the head wounds on these corpses. On both the river banks, there were heavily wooded forests, and who knew from where these dead men had come, or where they had been killed by these thugs and then brought here to be buried in the river mud. I have never seen the police come to investigate these deaths, nor have I seen anybody from the village go and put in a complaint in the police station. Who would take on such a trouble! They have only heard throughout their lives that the police were best left alone—it was dangerous to even edge near their boundaries. One might come back from the tiger's maw alive by God's grace, but never from their hands. Therefore, if anyone did come across such a sight, they would quietly move away elsewhere. At nightfall, the roaming hordes of jackals would celebrate a grand feast, and then go home after washing their mouths in the river water and all traces of the dead body would have disappeared.

Perhaps, one day, I would have also ended up like that,

but such a fate did not befall me. Let me tell you that story.

I was then around twelve. On the morning of a holiday, I was hiding in a room and making kites, when suddenly I heard a voice from the other neighbourhood—it was Nayan Baagdi's. He was telling my grandmother, 'Didithakrun[1], please give me around five rupees. I will repay the debt by feeding your grandson milk.'

Thakurma[2] loved Nayanchand dearly, and she merely asked, 'What will you do with five rupees, Nayan?'

He replied, 'I will buy a nice cow, Didi. My Pishima's[3] house is in Vasantpur; my cousin brother has sent me word that he is not being able to take care of four to five cows, and that he will give me one. I know he will not take any payment, but it would be wise to take care of four to five on me.'

My grandmother didn't say anything more but brought five rupees and gave it to him. He left after making an obeisance.

I had heard that in Vasantpur one can find nice fishing rods, and so I silently followed him. One had to follow a dirt track for about two miles, after which one took the Grand Trunk Road to Vasantpur. After walking for a mile, for some reason Nayan suddenly looked back and spotted me. He was furious at first, and then he offered to cut my fishing rods for me, but I had absolutely no desire to return home. I begged and pleaded but he paid no heed to me. He brought me back forcibly. My grandmother softened a little in the face of my

---

[1] Honorific for senior matriarchs
[2] Paternal grandmother
[3] Paternal aunt

tears, but Nayanchand would just not agree to take me. He said, 'Didi, it is not more than eight krosh both ways; it will be a moonlit night. I would have taken him happily, but the road is not good, there is fear of danger. If I cannot get back in time, then how will I, alone, manage the boy, the cow and myself—what will I do, you tell me, Didi?'

Everyone in this region knew why traversing roads after dark spelt fear. Grandmother put her foot down, and said, 'No, absolutely not. If you run away, I shall write to your schoolmaster and he will give you fifty lashes with the cane.'

Left with no other alternative, I devised another plan. After Nayan left, I said I would go down to the pond for a bath, massaged oil on my body, swung my towel over my shoulder, and set out. I ran through the mango and jackfruit orchards, through the forests growing on the riverside, and after two and a half miles of running, finally came and stood at the point where our little dirt road merged with the highway. After some ten minutes, I saw Nayan approaching. He scolded me terribly at first, and then, when he heard how I had come, he started laughing. He said, 'Let's go, *Thakur*,[4] whatever fate has in store for us will happen anyway. I cannot go back, now that I have come so far.'

Nayan-da bought rice-crisps, sugared rice-puffs and sugar crystals from a shop in Satgaon, and bundled it all into the corner of my dhoti. I munched my way through it as we walked, and it was nearly noon when we finally reached Nayan-da's Pishima's house in Vasantpur. Pishima was quite comfortable financially. Just beneath their house ran the Kunti river, small,

---

[4]Here, it is ambiguous whether Thakur refers to the Almighty or to the reverent form of address towards the little boy since he is a Brahmin.

but quite deep; high and low tides came in. After I had a bath, their eldest daughter-in-law made arrangements for me to have a meal of flattened rice, milk, jaggery and bananas on a banana leaf.[5] After I had finished eating, Nayan-da's Pishima suggested, 'He is just a kid, he has walked four to five krosh on the road, and he will have to walk back again. Let him sleep for now, and when it gets a little cooler, he can set out for home.' Her youngest son went off to cut fishing rods for me.

Both Nayan-da and I were so tired after our long walk that we woke up well after four o'clock. Nayan-da looked a little worried when he noted how late in the afternoon it was, but he did not make any comment. We left within ten minutes. Before he left, he tried to give his Pishima the five rupees, but she refused to accept it. She said, 'Buy sugar crystals for your children.'

On my shoulder was the bundle of fish rods, the cow's rope was held in Nayan-da's left hand, while his right held a four-feet high bamboo lathi. But one could not walk fast with a cow: and after just two krosh, the evening turned to night, and the moon rose in the skies. On both sides of the road there were huge peepal, banyan and pakur trees which formed a continuous canopy over the road. The road was dark, and only a dull moonlight gleamed through the leaves and fell on the road in patches. Nayan-da said, 'Dadabhai, you come to my left, and hold the cow's rope in your left hand, then I will be on your right.'

'Why Nayan-da?'

'Just like that, no reason. Come let's go.'

---

[5]The narrator is a Brahmin child and cannot take cooked food from the hands of lower castes.

Even though I was a child, I understood that Nayan-da's voice was full of anxiety.

Gradually, we left the metalled road and began to walk on the dirt path. The dense forests began to press even more heavily on both sides of the road; many ancient and really enormous pakur trees had formed such a thick and uninterrupted veil overhead that not even a sliver of moonlight could penetrate it. The young cowherds had led their herds through these paths in the evening not so long ago, the dust from their hooves was still heavy in the air, and getting into our noses and eyes—at such a moment, from some fifty to sixty feet away there came a heart-rending cry from a human voice: 'Baba go[6], they are killing me; whoever is there, come, save me!' Immediately there were accompanying sounds of lathis smashing down repeatedly. Then everything went quiet.

Nayan-da stood stock-still and then uttered, 'Ahh! It's all over!'

'What is over, Nayan-da?'

'A human being.' So saying he stood and thought, God knows what for a while, and then he said, 'Come Dadabhai, let us go ahead a little carefully.'

The cow to my left, Nayan-da to my right, and me in between the two. I have heard many things since childhood, I have seen certain things on my own account, and so, child though I was, I understood completely what was going on. The appeal, 'Whoever is there, come, save me!' was still ringing in my ears, and I said in a frightened voice, 'But Nayan-da, they are all standing in front of us, how will we go ahead?

---

[6]'Baba go', almost equivalent to 'oh dear' refers to a loud utterance following an experience of acute pain.

What if they kill us?'

'No, Dadabhai, they will not dare to hit us while I am here. They are thangarays—they will run away before us. They are big cowards.'

The three of us—the cow, myself and Nayanchand, began to edge forward slowly. My legs were shaking in terror; my condition was such that I could not breathe. So far nothing had been visible under the dense shadow of the trees and the dust, but as we moved forward another fifteen to twenty feet, we suddenly glimpsed some five to six men running and hiding behind the trunk of a pakur tree. Nayan-da suddenly stopped dead and yelled—what a terrible voice that was—'*Khabardar*, I say to you all! There is a Brahmin boy with me. You dare throw the pabada at us and I will not leave a single man alive, and so I am warning you!'

No one answered. We went a little further and then saw that a man was lying face down on the ground. A few rays of moonlight had fallen on the still figure—Nayan-da bent down to look, and then broke into loud lamentations! Blood was flowing from his nose, ears and mouth—his legs were still trembling with departing life. The beggar's bag was still slung on his shoulder, but the rice-grains gathered after a day's begging had spilled out, mixing with the dust. The *ektara*[7] from his hand, broken by the blows from the lathis, had been flung a little distance away.

Nayan-da straightened up and said, 'You hellhounds! You worms from hell! You killed a Vaishnav[8] for nothing? What

[7]A single-stringed musical instrument with the sound-box made of dried gourd.

[8]A sect of mendicants who formed a religious community in Nabadwip of

have you done?' His harsh voice of a few moments ago had now filled with pain and sorrow.

But there was no sound from the other side. The chief reason for Nayan-da's sorrow was that he himself was a Vaishnav. He always had thick tulsi beads hanging from his neck, while on his nose there was always the tilak, and all over his body a variety of marks. He had a small prayer-room in his house, where the *shripad* of the Mahaprabhu had been established. He did not touch water without meditating on the given *Ishtonaam*[9] a thousand times. He had been acquainted with letters in the village *pathshala* when he was a boy; now, with his own efforts he could easily read large print. Everyday, he read the cheap Battala editions[10] of the Vaishnav religious scriptures for many hours right into the night by lamplight. He did not touch meat, and sometime in the future, he hoped to give up fish as well.

There is a small history to his becoming a Vaishnav; let me recount that story here. Now he was close to forty, but when he was twenty-five to thirty, he had been involved in some case of robbery and had spent a year as an undertrial prisoner in jail. My grandmother's cousin brother (her father's sister's son) was a well-known lawyer in the region; with his

---

Nadia (a district in the state of West Bengal) under the spiritual guidance of Chaitanyadev (also known as Mahaprabhu) in sixteenth-century Bengal at the peak of the Bhakti movement, and he is represented by the icon in the form of holy feet (*shripad*). The followers of this sect (called *boshtam* in the dialect) generally sing and dance in celebration of faith for the cowherd Krishna (who is also the Godhead Vishnu).

[9]Sacred and secret name given to the faithful by the Guru during initiation,

[10]Battala is a road near College Street in Calcutta where vernacular printing presses brought out cheap editions.

help and by spending a lot of money and effort, she had managed to free him. As soon as he emerged from the police lockup, he went straight to Nabadwip, and was initiated into Vaishnavism by some Goswami there, and he returned to his own locality with his head shaven, big tulsi beads round his neck, a die-hard Vaishnav. Nayan would come and stretch out in obeisance to my grandmother whenever he felt like it. As he had no right to touch a Brahmin's widow, he would pluck a leaf from a tree and place it near her feet, she would touch it with her big toe, and then he would place the leaf reverently on his forehead and neck, and say, 'Didithakrun, bless me so that I am reborn in an honest caste, that I can take the dust from your feet with my hands.' Thakurma would say lovingly, 'Nayan, I bless you so that you are reborn as a Brahmin.'

Nayan's eyes would fill with tears and he would say, 'I do not hope for so much Didi, there is no end to my sins, I have hidden nothing from you.'

Thakurma would reassure him, 'All that has been expiated, Nayan. How many people in this world are as devoted, completely immersed in their belief in the Bhagwat[11], as you are? Never move away from this path, and you would not have to worry about your afterlife.'

As Nayan would leave, wiping his eyes, Thakurma would call after him, 'Tomorrow, don't forget to take some prasad.'

I have seen all this many times with my own eyes. It was but natural that the Vaishnav's cruel death, the very symbol to which he had devoted his whole life, had really moved and angered Nayan. He said, 'What did you expect to gain from a poor Vaishnav beggar who was returning home after

---

[11]As a devout Vaishnav to be immersed in the name of Narayan or Krishna.

begging the whole day? A couple of pice at the most? I feel like beating you all to death.'

Now from the shadows under the trees came an answer, 'Who gives even two pice? It is the combined fortunes of your fourteen generations that you are escaping with your life this time. Don't give us religious advice—get lost, quick!'

Before these words were said, Nayan roared like a tiger, 'Indeed, you bastard! Run? Fearing you?' He then took out the five rupees, allowed them to fall tinkling into his outstretched palm, and challenged, 'Don't let so much money go untaken, that's my advice. If you can, come together and take them. But let me warn you again, if my Babathakur gets scratched by a blade of grass, I will not go home until I make all of you bite the dust of the road for ever. I am Shetla's Nayan Chhaati, no one else. Have you heard of the name, or do you just roam around with lathis in your hands killing helpless beggars? Worthless sons of jackals and dogs!'

Complete silence under the tree. Nayan stayed still for the space of two minutes, and then said even more harshly, 'What—are you going to come or do I return home with the money safely tucked into my waistband?'

No answer. There were a few pabadas lying on the road, Nayan picked them up one by one, and said, 'Come dada, let's go home. Your grandmother must be getting really worried. Those are just sons of jackals and dogs, they will not come near human beings. If you chased them with that bunch of fishing rods, they would all run away Dadabhai!'

By now, my fear had given way to returning courage—I said, 'Shall I run after them Nayan-da?'

Nayan could not help laughing, and said, 'Let it be dada, there is no need. They might bite.'

Again we began to walk on. But Nayan fell strangely silent, he did not answer a single one of my questions. He suddenly came to a stop under the shadow of a big tree, and said, 'No, Dadabhai, after seeing that with my own eyes, I won't let it go like that. I will avenge the death of that Brahmin-Vaishnav.'

'How will you take revenge, Nayan-da?'

'I will be able to catch at least one. Then you and I will beat him to death.'

At the prospect of beating someone to death, I was transported with joy. It was a new type of game. Whatever terrible things I had heard about them had been nothing but a pack of lies. Nayan-da had not allowed me to go after them, otherwise I would have certainly chased them and managed to catch at least one. I declared, 'Nayan-da, you must hold one fellow firmly, I will beat him to death. But what if my fishing rod breaks?'

Nayan laughed again and said, 'Fishing rods will not kill him dada, take this lathi.' And he put into my hands one of the pabadas he had collected and told me, 'You stand here holding the cow, Dadabhai; I will soon capture and bring you one or two of them. But don't you be scared if you hear screaming and crying.'

'Naah! Why fear? There is a stick in my hand!'

Nayan put two more pabadas under his arm, with his right hand held the big lathi, and then began to crawl on all fours towards the crime zone, but not on the road, along the edge of the forest. The thangarays had thought we had left. They were rifling through the belongings of the dead beggar, searching for goodies.

Suddenly, one of them caught sight of Nayan standing a little distance away behind a tree. He cried out with fright,

'Who's there?'

'I, Nayan Chhati. Stand there! If you dare to run away, you will die.'

But before he could finish the sentence, I heard the sound of many running feet, and following hard upon it, with a muffled shriek, someone tumbling with a crash into the bushes.

Nayan shouted across to me, 'I have caught one of the fellows, the rest have run off.'

I began to jump on the spot at the good news. I called out to him, 'Catch him and bring him here, I will beat him to death. Don't you kill him.'

'No, dada, you will do the killing.'

There was another pathetic wail, possibly caused by the jab of Nayan's lathi. After a minute or two, I saw a man come limping towards us, with Nayanchand just behind. As soon as he was close, he burst into tears and wrapped his arms around my legs. Nayan pulled him to his feet. Now that I actually got to see him, I shuddered with aversion. His face was smeared with blacking, with big, white, dabs of lime. He was as tall as he was thin, and he wore a tattered loincloth. He was still weeping. Nayan dealt him a huge slap across his cheek and said, 'Be quiet, bastard! Answer all my questions truthfully. How many of you were there? What are their names, where do they live?'

At first the man did not want to say anything, but after a hard prod to his back, he reeled off their names and addresses. Nayan said, 'I will remember, I will not forget. Now tell me, after *boshtamthakur* fell down, you dealt him how many blows?'

'It might have been five or seven.'

Nayan said between his teeth, 'Fine, let it be five or seven. Now lie down just the way I saw boshtamthakur lying down.

Dadabhai, come forward. Mind, you have to dispatch him with just five to seven blows with that pabada. Let's see the power of your arm. You fellow, what are you waiting for? Lie down!' And he pulled down the man to a sitting posture on the road by his ears. Before he could lie down himself, Nayan threw him onto the dusty road with two or three tremendous kicks on his back. He said, 'Do not delay dada, aim for the head and hit hard. It shouldn't take more than two to three blows.'

Nayan-da's voice had changed completely, his face belonged to someone else. His transformed appearance smote me with a chill of fear. Instead of starting a new game, my hands and feet began to shake uncontrollably, and I said tearfully, 'I cannot, Nayan-da.'

'You cannot? Then I will finish him off.'

'No, Nayan-da, no, don't kill him.'

However, ever since the man had fallen under the kicks, he had remained motionless. He had not even begged for his life—he was silent.

I said, 'Come, let's tie him up and take him to the thana.'

At this, suddenly Nayan-da started and said, 'In the thana? In the hands of the police?'

'Yes. He has killed a man, and so they should hang him. As you sow, so shall you reap.'

Nayan was quiet for a while; then he prodded the man with his lathi, and said, 'Hey, get up!'

But there was no response. Nayan said, 'Has the fellow died or what? The weakling—for two days perhaps he has not even had a fistful of rice—and he has hit the road to beat people to death! Go fellow, get lost! Get up and go home!' But the man remained totally still. Nayan then bent down, held his hand near his nose, and said, 'No he is not dead. He is just unconscious. When he comes to, he will go home by himself. Come dada, let us also go home. It is now very late, your grandmother will be so worried.'

As we resumed our journey, I said, 'Why did you let him go Nayan-da? It would have served him right if we had given him up to the police.'

'Why Dadabhai?'

'He would have been hanged and good riddance. It is written in our books that if you murder anybody, you are hanged for it.'

'Is it indeed, dada?'

'Of course it is. Come home with me, I will open the book and show you.'

Nayan pretended to be surprised and said, 'What are you saying, dada—a man will be killed if he killed a man?'

'Yes, indeed. That will be his just punishment. That is what we have read.'

Nayan smiled a little and said, 'But all that is written cannot be realized in this world, dadabhai.'

'Why not, Nayan-da?'

Nayan did not answer at once. He thought for a while before he said, 'Perhaps because everyone in the world cannot put other people into police custody.'

I never got to know that day why some people were unable to do this, why they committed such wrongdoing, and even today I do not know why. Still, while walking on, I kept ruminating over this, and I again asked, 'But Nayan-da, after they go back they will kill people again, won't they?'

Nayan said, 'No, dada, that they will not. Till I live, they will never do such a thing again.'

I could not be completely satisfied with this answer. I

preferred that they be hanged. I said, 'But they are still alive. They have gone unpunished.'

Thinking deeply about something else, Nayan absentmindedly answered, 'Who knows, perhaps one day they will be punished.' Then suddenly coming back to himself, he said, 'I don't know the answer to that Dadabhai, your grandmother knows. When you grow up, you must ask her one day.'

But I could not wait to grow up. The moment I put a foot inside the house, I burst into speech with suitable gesticulations of all my limbs, and poured forth the story of our victory over the thangarays and all the stirring events that had followed our purchase of a cow, of course omitting such irrelevant details like trembling hands and legs. Thakurma listened to me with great attention, and then she heaved a sigh and held me close without saying a word.

Nayan was listening quietly all this while. After I had finished telling my story, he took out the five rupees and placed them near Thakurma's feet, and said, 'I got the cow for free. Your money has returned to you didi. Neither did Pishima take it, nor did your daughter-in-law's brothers[12] on the way.'

Thakurma smiled a little, 'When I see my daughter-in-law, I shall tell her. But even I will not take those five rupees— you can use it for making food offerings to your god. But Nayan, let me say one thing—you still have not succeeded in becoming a good Vaishnav.'

'Why didi?'

'Do they lure people by clinking money together?

---

[12]In the original, the term *sala*, a kinship term for one's wife's brothers, isn't used since it is also a term of abuse; further, in front of an elderly and high-caste person, not using it is a sign of respect as was befitting of those times.

Supposing they had rushed at you, unable to control their greed?'

'Then another five to six people would have died. But didi, how little would that have added to the huge burden of sin already weighing on Nayan?'

Grandmother was quiet. She knew the significance of these words, and so did Nayan himself. But he too did not say anything more. He merely paid his obeisance to her from afar, picked up the five rupees and left the place silently.

six

CHILDHOOD MEMORIES*

ONE

*A*t the time of my *annaprasan*[1], when I had not quite managed the feat of truly becoming myself, and perhaps also because my honoured grandfather had not quite mastered the principles of astrology, I became 'Sukumar'. It did not take long—just two to four years—for my grandfather to realize that there was not much in common between me and my name. Now, skipping over the next twelve to thirteen years, I will narrate the next part of the story. Certainly, not many persons will properly appreciate these revealing nuggets of self-introduction; nevertheless, look, our household was (located) in the village, and I have been there since my childhood. My honoured father used to work somewhere in the western regions. I seldom visited him. I stayed with my grandmother

---

*Translated from the original 'Balyo-Smriti', in *SSS*, Vol. 2, pp. 1693–98.
[1] A Hindu ritual that celebrates the first intake of solid food by a baby at his reaching six months of age.

in the village. There were no limits to my pranks at home. In short, I was a little Ravana. When my old grandfather would complain, 'What are you turning into? You don't listen to anybody. Now I will write a letter to your father', I would reply with a slight smile: 'Those days are gone. I do not fear even my father's father. If my grandmother is with me, where's the need to fear?' She would then jokingly twit grandfather, 'How was the answer? Will you take him on again?'

In case my revered grandfather, in extreme irritation, did manage to write a letter to my father, I would immediately hide his box of opium. Until he tore up the letter, I would refuse to disgorge the box. In the face of such attacks, especially the threat to his source of addiction, my grandfather did not tell me off much. I, too, flourished happily.

But what of that? There is a limit set to all happiness. Inevitably, it happened to me too. Grandfather's paternal cousin (son of his younger uncle), Gobindo-babu, had always worked in Allahabad. Now he received his pension and came to live at home. Along with him came his grandson, Srijukta Rajaninath, who had passed his BA. I call him Mejodada. Before this, there had not been much interaction with him as he did not frequent these parts. Moreover, they lived in a different house. If he did pay a visit, he did not inquire after me. If he happened to meet me by chance, our interchange was limited to 'Hey there, how are you? What are you studying?'

But now he came and settled down in the village for good. And therefore, I was tracked down and made to account for myself. In just a couple of days' of socialization, he tamed me to such an extent that the moment I would see him, I would feel scared, my face would fall, my heart would start thumping—as if I was indeed guilty of many crimes and for which I would receive much punishment. And in truth, I used to be thus guilty those days. Every day, somehow, I felt impelled to commit some crime or the other. A couple of misdeeds, a daily quota of two to four instances of misbehaviour were fairly standard for me. However, even though I feared my elder brother, I loved him deeply. I have erred grievously even with him, but he has never taken me to task; and if he did say something, I could brush it off with a casual—'it is only Mejodada, he will forget everything in a little while'.

If Mejodada had so desired, he might have corrected my characteristic waywardness, but he did not. Now that he had settled down in the village, there was a slight restriction on my freedom, but nevertheless, I was still reasonably satisfied with life.

Every day, I would consume a paisa worth of grandfather's tobacco. The poor old man, dreading my raids, would attempt to hide the tobacco next to the leg of the bed, in the hidden drawer in the divan, in the space between the rafters, but I would hunt it out, and consume it. I was fine, I ate, flew kites, not bothered with rubbish; I had almost abandoned studies. I would kill birds, I would catch and roast squirrels, and eat them, look for rabbits in the rabbit holes in the forests, and suffered no worries.

My father used to work in Buxar. From there he came to neither keep an eye on me nor thrash me. I have already narrated the condition of my grandparents. Therefore, in short, I was doing fine.

One day, when I had come back from my afternoon ramble, I heard from my grandmother that I would have to go live with my Mejodada in Calcutta to study. After polishing off my meal, armed with a measure of tobacco, I went to my grandfather and asked, 'I have to go to Calcutta?' He said, 'Yes.' I had concluded beforehand that all this was just my grandfather's cunning ploy. I called his bluff—'If I go at all, I will go today.' Grandfather smiled and said, 'Why are you worrying, dada? Rajani is going to Calcutta today. All the arrangements for living there have already been made, he will leave this very day.' I grew red hot with rage. As it was, I had not managed to unearth his secret hoard of tobacco—the one measure I had found would not be enough for even one satisfactory pull. On top of that, this! I felt cheated: but after issuing an ultimatum, one could not take it back. And thus I found myself on my way to Calcutta. As I bent down to touch grandfather's feet at the time of our departure, I said to myself, 'Hari, I wish that I come back to attend your funeral by tomorrow. After that I will see who dares to pack me off to Calcutta.'

TWO

This was my first visit to Calcutta. I have never seen such a huge, thrumming city before. I thought to myself, if just at the midpoint of the wooden bridge over the enormous Ganges, or just where those ships stood with their masts pointing to the sky, I happened to fall in and drown, then I would never be able to go back home. I did not like Calcutta one bit. How could one love something which caused so much fear? That I could ever love it, I could not say with confidence.

Where had that old river bank (of the village), that clump of bamboos, the *bael* tree in the middle of the commons, the *jamrul* tree in the corner of the house belonging to the Mittirs'—disappeared? There was absolutely nothing here. There were only huge houses, huge cars, horses and people jostling each other, people shoving each other, big roads; there was not even a small garden at the back of the house where I could smoke a measure of tobacco in peace. I felt like crying. I wiped my eyes and thought, God has given life, he will provide food [for the soul].

I am now admitted into a Calcutta school; I study well, and so nowadays, I am a '"good" boy'. Of course, back home, my name is famous as…but let that pass.

We—a group of friends and kin—live together in a mess[2]. In our mess, there are four people—Mejodada, Ram-babu, Jagannath-babu, and I. Ram-babu and Jagannath-babu are Mejodada's friends. Apart from them, there is also a servant and a Brahmin cook.

Gadadhar was our cook. He was older to me by some three to four years. I have never encountered such a good person. I did not have any friends in the locality. Even though Gadadhar's nature was utterly different from mine, he became my greatest friend.

There was no end to the stories he and I used to exchange. His home was in a village in Midnapur district. I used to love listening to the stories of his boyhood, to the stories of his village. I have heard these stories so many times that I am sure I will be able to find my way about in that place blindfolded. On Sundays, I used to go for a stroll with him in Gader Math[3]. In the evenings, we locked the kitchen door

---

[2] An urban, rented boarding facility for people who needed to reside in Calcutta, but did not want to buy or rent a house in the city.

[3] A huge park established by the British in Calcutta in the nineteenth century. It had become a promenade for the British ruling class and the Bengali gentry alike.

and played *binti*.[4] After our meals, we would smoke together from his little hubble-bubble. We always used to work together. For me, there was no other friend—companion, chum, buddy, friend, Bhulo, Kelo, Khoka, Khanda of Muchi-*paadaa*[5]—he was all those rolled into one for me. I have never heard him speak in a rough tone. People would abuse him without any reason; while my entire being would burn with anger, he never uttered a word of protest—as if he was indeed guilty of some wrongdoing.

After feeding everyone, he would seat himself in a corner of the kitchen with his small plate of food, and, even if I had a hundred tasks, I would manage to be present. There was often, to his misfortune, almost nothing left—so much so, that even the rice was in short supply. I have never been present while somebody's been eating—I have never before witnessed that during a meal, there has been a shortage of rice, a shortage of vegetables, a shortage of fish. I used to feel quite strange.

During my childhood, my grandmother would occasionally say sadly, 'The boy has become shrivelled and rope-thin as he only eats a near-starvation diet—how will he survive!' But I just could not manage to eat what, in my grandmother's definition, was a non-starvation diet. Whether I became shrivelled or rope-like, I preferred to eat a near-starvation diet. It was only after coming to Calcutta that I have understood that there was a world of difference between that and this near-starvation diet. Before this, I have never felt that if anybody did not get enough to eat, tears could spring to my eyes. Before this,

---

[4] A card game
[5] Locality

I have thrown water, contaminated by another mouth, on my grandfather while he ate, and successfully prevented him from eating further. I have flung an infant covered in poo at my grandmother and prevented her from eating further. They have gone without a meal, but tears have not come to my eyes. Grandfather, grandmother—they are my dear kin, venerable, and they have a deep affection for me; I have never felt sorrow for them. I have kept them half-hungry and kept them so through my machinations with a deep satisfaction. And for this Gadadhar—a nobody from nowhere—tears spring unbidden to my eyes.

I cannot understand what has happened to me after I have come to Calcutta. I also cannot imagine from where such enormous quantity of tears come into my eyes. Nobody has seen me weep. During my childhood, my preceptor has broken a cane of date-leaf on my back, but his wish to see me dissolve into tears has remained unfulfilled. The boys would say, 'Sukumar's body is made of stone.' I would say to myself, 'It is not my body—my mind is made of stone.' I do not burst into tears like a baby. Indeed, I used to feel ashamed of tears, and I still do, but I cannot control myself. Furtively, checking to see if the coast is clear, like a guilty thief—I wipe my eyes a couple of times. On my way to school, I see a bunch of people begging—either one is missing a hand, or one missing a leg, yet another missing both his eyes; in fact, I cannot even enumerate the variety of missing parts these beggars are inflicted with. I have known only those who, tilaks on their foreheads, with *khanjanis*[6] in their hands, sing *'joy radhey'*—what kind of beggars were these? In deep anguish,

---

[6]Metal castanets

I would say in my heart, 'Dear God, send these beggars to our village.' Forget the hapless beggars, let me come back to my own tale.

So though my eyes grew used to the sights of Calcutta, I could not quite achieve the character of Vidyasagar. Now and then Maa Saraswati[7] from back home would mount on my shoulders without any warning. Under her command, the kind of good deeds I would be impelled to commit has created within me a lasting disgust for that Goddess. I would be on the lookout for wreaking mayhem on any victim my choice alighted on. Ram-babu had carefully pleated his black-bordered desi dhoti for three hours flat for his evening promenade. At the right moment, I got hold of the dhoti, stretched it out to its former unpleated state and left it there. In the evening he took one look at the dhoti and collapsed. My delight knew no bounds. Jagannath-babu was late for his office, he was hurriedly sitting down to eat, with no moment to spare. I, at the right moment, cut off all the buttons of his office robe. Before leaving for school, I peeped in once to see that Jagannath-babu was on the verge of crying loudly. I laughed all the way to the school in sheer joy. In the evening, Jagannath-babu came back from office and complained, 'That rascal Gada has cut off the buttons of my office robe and has sold them—turn the rascal out.' Both my Mejodada and Ram-babu smiled a little at the anecdote of the robe. Mejodada observed, 'There

[7]Goddess Saraswati/Binapani as *Vac*, occasionally has been used by the Gods to confound intelligence. Kumbhakarna, Ravana's brother, was similarly confounded by her, and so he asked for a boon of *nidra* or sleep, for six months, after which he would wake for a day, eat enormous amounts of food and then relapse into slumber for another six months. Saratchandra's protagonist is referring to this Saraswati.

are so many kinds of thieves, but I have never heard of any who steals the buttons of a robe to sell them.' Jagannath-babu, angrier than ever, charged, 'The rogue did not take them in the morning, did not take them in the afternoon, did not take them at night, but took them just before I was leaving for office. I had a real run of misfortune today—I had to go into the office in a torn black *piran*.'[8]

Everyone laughed. Even Jagannath-babu. Only I could not laugh. I felt nervous lest Gadadhar was gotten rid of. He was such a dunce, perhaps he would take all the blame on his own shoulders. Perhaps Mejodada had an inkling as to who had taken the buttons. There was no pressure on the poverty-stricken Gadadhar. But I promised to myself that I would never commit any deed that might put someone else at risk.

I have never before made such a promise, I do not know if I would ever have made such a promise. However, that Gadadhar has actually been the end of me.

How a person's character gets corrected is beyond anybody's comprehension. No effort of my preceptor, of my grandfather, or of any other venerable authority-figure had succeeded in wringing from me such a promise. But I made such a promise by simply thinking of the cook Gadadhar's face. I do not know if that promise has ever been unconsciously broken, but I have never, in memory, broken it deliberately.

Now, let me talk of another person. He is our servant Rama. By caste, Rama is either a Kayastha or Sadgop[9]—something like that. I do not know where his home is, at least I have not

---

[8] A casual, half-sleeved, cotton upper garment normally worn at home.
[9] Service caste, clean lower caste

heard of it. It is certainly rare to come across such a careful and highly efficient servant. And if I ever come across such a one again, I will certainly ask him where his home is.

I used to see Rama spin around like a top, performing domestic work. Now Rama is washing clothes; right away I see Mejodada has readied himself for a bath and Rama is scrubbing his body; immediately after, he is mighty busy with betel leaves and areca nuts. He is constantly moving around in this manner. For Mejodada, he is 'The favourite! A great man!' But I could not stand him. For that rascal, I used to face Mejodada's ire often. Especially, he used to constantly discomfit poor Gada. I disliked him intensely. But what could come of it? He was Mejodada's 'favourite!' Ram-babu of our mess could not stand him either. He used to call him 'The rogue!' Though he felt unable to explain the true nature of this name-tag, the two of us knew that his annoyance with 'the rogue' had plenty of solid reasons. His biggest grouse was that Rama used to pass himself off as 'Ram-babu' in his self-introductions. Even Mejodada occasionally called him Ram-babu. Our Ram-babu used to hold such liberties in deep disapproval. Enough of this rubbish—one evening, Mejodada returned home with a lamp he had purchased. It was a very good product, costing some fifty to sixty rupees. When everybody had left for their evening strolls, I called Gadadhar and showed him the lamp. Gadadhar had never seen such a light. He was highly thrilled and he touched it a couple of times; then he left for the kitchen to continue with his work. But my curiosity refused to die. How do I open the chimney? How do I see the mechanism inside? I turned it over and examined it many times; I made many attempts to rotate it, but it just refused to open. After a lot of observation, I noticed that there was a screw set below, and so I turned and twisted it a bit. Suddenly, the entire top half came loose. I could not catch it in my flurry, and the lamp's glass dome fell from the table and shattered into pieces.

THREE

That night I came back home late from a walk. Upon my return, I found that the whole house was reverberating with angry voices. Everyone had ringed Gadadhar around, and he was crouching in the centre. Mejodada was extremely angry. Gadadhar was being cross-examined.

Tears were streaming from Gadadhar's eyes. He was saying 'Babu, I had certainly touched it, but I have not broken it. Sukumar-babu showed it to me—I also looked at it. Then he went for a walk, I too went to cook.'

Nobody believed his version. It was decided that he had broken the chimney. Some of his salary was still due: a chimney worth three rupees and fifty paise came from that money and in the evening the lamp was lit. Everyone was happy. But my eyes burnt with tears. I kept thinking about the fact that I had stolen from him three rupees and fifty paise. I could not stay there a moment longer. I wept and got Mejodada's permission and straightaway returned home. I had decided to take the money from grandmother and return not three rupees and fifty paise but seven rupees to Gadadhar, in secret. I had no money at that time. All the money used to be with Mejodada. And therefore, to get the money I needed to come home. I had imagined that I would not stay for more than a day. But it did not transpire that way. Seven to eight days slipped by.

After seven to eight days, I entered the mess in Calcutta. The moment I entered, I called out, 'Gada'. There was no response. I called again, 'Gadadharthakur!'

Now Ramacharan came up and said, 'Chhotobabu, when did you arrive?'

'Just now—where is Thakur?'

'Thakur! Not here.'

'Where has he gone?'

'Babu has turned him out!'

'Turned him out! Why?'

'Because he had been thieving.'

At first, I could not quite understand what was being said, and so I continued staring at Rama's face. Rama gauged the state of my mind and said with a slight smile, 'Chhotobabu, you are surprised, but you did not know him. Therefore, you loved him so much. He was quiet and sly; I saw through his butter-will-not-melt-in-the-mouth act.'

How he was quiet and sly and how I had not figured out his butter-will-not-melt-in-the-mouth act, were things I just could not comprehend. I asked, 'Whose money had he stolen?'

'Mejobabu's.'

'Where was it?'

'In the pocket of his shirt.'

'How much money?'

'Four rupees.'

'Who had seen him take it?'

'Nobody had actually seen him take it, but it is a kind of seeing nevertheless.'

'Why?'

'Is it something to ask? You were not at home, Ram-babu had not taken it, Jagannath-babu had not taken it, I had not taken it. Then who took it? Where did it go?'

'Then you had caught him?'

Rama laughed and said, 'Who else?'

You can all safely buy Thhonthhone sandals. I do not think such tough durable sandals are produced anywhere else[10].

FOUR

I went to the kitchen and burst into tears. That little hubble-bubble had dust on it. Nobody had touched it these four or five days, nobody had changed the water filter. Written in coal on one side of the wall was, 'Chhotobabu, I have been thieving. I am leaving this place. If I am alive, I shall come back.'

I was young then. With the emotions of a young boy, I tightly held the hubble-bubble close to my chest and began to cry. Why, what for—I had no answers to these questions.

My heart was no longer in that mess. In the evening, I would come back from a walk and enter the kitchen once. I would see someone else cooking and I would go to my own room and open my books to study. At certain times, I could not stand even Mejodada. Even the rice tasted bitter. Several days later, one night I asked Mejodada, 'Mejodada! What have you done?'

'What, what have I done?'

'Gada could never have stolen your money.'

Everyone knew that I used to be very fond of Gadathakur. Mejodada said, 'I did not do a good thing, Sukumar. Whatever has happened has happened, but why did you thrash Rama so badly?'

'I am not sorry I did. Will you turn me out too?'

---

[10]Thhonthhone sandals were made from very tough leather and very firmly stitched, for they had not broken when Sukumar had used them to thrash Rama. The young employer and others of his class considered beating a servant quite normal. Saratchandra also seems to think that this beating is justified.

Mejodada had never heard such words from me. I demanded, 'How much did you manage to raise out of him?'

Dada became very sad and replied, 'I did not do a good thing. I had deducted all his salary and managed to get two rupees and fifty paise from him. I had not intended to go so far.'

Whenever I used to go for a walk, if I saw a man with a dirty cloth over his shoulder in torn sandals in the distance, I used to run after him in order to see his face. What can I say about the kind of inchoate hope that used to build up every day, and every day it would turn to hopelessness!

After almost five months, there arrived a money-order in Dada's name—a money order for one rupee and fifty paise. That day I saw Dada wipe his eyes. The coupon is still with me.

Many years have passed by. But even today, that poverty-stricken Gadadhar still occupies a half of my heart.

section two

seven

THE MEMORIES OF DEOGHAR[*]

*I*had come to Deoghar for a change of air and at the doctor's command. As I was on my way, a few lines by Rabindranath Tagore were constantly running through my mind—

> *Ashudhey-daktare,*
> *byadhir cheyey aadhi holo bodo.*
> *Jokhon korley asthi jorojoro,*
> *tokhon bolley hawa bodol koro.*

What with medicines and the doctor,
The penny counted more than the disease.
When even my bones felt tired,
Then he advised me to get a change of air.

People are well aware of the actual benefits from a change of air, but they still come. Even I have done so. I stay in a big house surrounded by a walled garden. From three in the

---

[*]Translated from the original 'Deogharer Smriti', in *SSS*, Vol. 2, pp. 1777–79.

morning someone close by begins to sing bhajans in a broken voice and in a monotonous tune. I wake up, open the door and sit outside. Slowly the darkness lifts and the birds begin to arrive. I noticed that the earliest amongst them was the *doel*. Even before the darkness had passed, they would begin their songs. Then gradually, one or two *bulbulis*, *shyamas*, *shaliks*, *tuntunis*—would begin their morning songs from the mango tree next door, from the *bakul* grove of this house, from the top of the *peepal* tree growing on the roadside. I could not see some of them but from their sounds, it felt like I knew each one of them. A pair of yellow *bene-bou* birds used to come a little late. They used to sit on top of the eucalyptus tree growing near the wall and announce their presence daily. Suddenly, for about two days, I missed them, and grew anxious—had they been caught? In this district there were no dearth of bird catchers. They did a business out of selling birds. However, on the third day when I saw them on their familiar perch, it felt like a genuine anxiety melting away.

The morning passes in this fashion. Late afternoon, I come and sit at the gate. I do not have the strength to walk about, but I like to see the people who can do so. I saw that among the middle-class householders, the women sufferers far outnumbered the men. A lot of young girls with swollen feet would go by first. I could make out they were victims of *beriberi*. The poor things used to take such great care to hide the embarrassment of their swollen feet. It was getting hot, socks were unsuitable, but some would wear tight socks on their feet. Some would wear saris right down to their feet—which would make walking difficult—but they wanted to hide their deformity from the curious eyes of strangers. I used to feel particularly sad when a girl from a poor household used to pass by. She would walk all by herself. She had no relatives with her, only three small children. She was somewhere between twenty-four to twenty-five, but her face was as drained of blood as her body was of flesh. She had no strength to drag her bloodless body forward, but still carried the youngest boy in her arms. He did not know how to walk, but there was no way she could leave him behind. That young woman had such tired eyes. It seemed as though she felt shy of me—she wanted to cross this stretch of road as quickly as possible. She used to cover her three children in torn clothes and take this route daily. Maybe she hoped that though nothing so far had helped, perhaps the healthy air of the Santhal Parganas and this wracking walk would accomplish the much-needed cure. She would be free of disease, and would get back her strength, her hopes, again she would be able to serve her husband and children and would fulfil her destiny as a woman. I would sit and often think in my own mind, this apart, what other wish could she have? She is a Bengali girl—who would have taught her to hope for anything beyond this? I used to bless her inwardly—let the young woman return home after regaining her health, let her have the strength and the opportunity to look after the three children who have completely drained her of all vitality. Whose daughter she was, whose wife, or where she stayed—I did not know but as a representative of the countless number of young women in Bengal, her image cast a profound impression upon my heart, which was not to be easily forgotten.

I had been accompanied by a young friend all the way here. His service to me was selfless. Just as I had seen him during the time I was extremely ill in Calcutta, here too I found him to be just the same. Sometimes he used to urge me, 'Dada, come on, let's go for a walk today.' I used to say, 'Bhai, you go, I can do that sitting here.' He used to get impatient and retort, 'There are many men here who are far older than you but who are busy taking walks. How will you get an appetite if you do not walk about a bit?' I used to say, 'If that is a little less, I can bear it, but I cannot bear roaming the roads without reason.'

He would go off on his own in some annoyance, but would warn me, 'Do not go back to the house on your own. Get the servants to fetch you a lamp. Here, the kraits are fairly abundant. Harmless species, except they do not like people stepping on them.'

That day my friend had gone off for his constitutional. Evening was as yet far off. I observed that some old men had managed to acquire an appetite, and were now stepping towards home as briskly as their health permitted them. Possibly, they were afflicted with rheumatism, and it was necessary that they got back home before dusk. I felt quite encouraged as I looked at their agility, and told myself, I should also go for a walk. That day I strolled through many a road for a long while. It had become dark, and I thought myself to be on my own, when I suddenly caught sight of a dog trotting along behind me. I asked him, 'Hello, will you come with me? Why don't you escort me through these dark streets to my house?' He stood a little way away wagging his tail. I understood he was willing. So I invited, 'Then come with me.' Under the light of a street lamp I saw that he was quite old, the hair from his back was missing in chunks because of disease, and he walked with a limp. But it was evident that in his youth he had been quite a powerful dog. I asked him a great many questions while the two of us walked to our gate. I opened the gate and issued him an invitation, 'Come in, today you are my guest.' He stood outside wagging his tail, but could not summon up enough courage to enter through the gate. The servant arrived with a lamp, and wanted to shut the gate, but I said, 'Let it remain open. If he comes in, give him something to eat.' When I enquired after an hour, I heard that he had not come in, he had gone off somewhere.

Next morning, the moment I came out I saw my guest of yesterday standing right outside the gate. I asked him, 'I invited you to a meal yesterday; why didn't you come?'

He wagged his tail in answer. I told him, 'Today you will eat here—don't leave without food. Got it?' In answer, he wagged his tail hard—perhaps meaning, 'Really? Are you truly asking me?'

At night, the servant came and informed me that the dog was sitting in the verandah under the portico. I called the Brahmin cook and informed him, 'He is my guest. Give him food to eat.'

The next morning I heard that the guest had not left. He had ignored the rules governing etiquette, and was sitting in peace and contentment. I said, 'Let it be, give him food.'

I knew that everyday a lot of food was wasted, and so no one would object. But there were objections and very serious objections at that. I did not know that the gardener's wife had a strong claim to whatever extra food there was. She was young and good looking, and was flexible about what she ate. The servants sympathized more with her cause. And therefore, my guest had to fast. Late afternoon, I moved down to the road, and saw that my guest was already sitting there amid the dust. When I went for a walk, he was my companion. When I asked him, 'So, my guest, how was the meat cooked today? What did chewing the bones taste like?' he answered by wagging his tail, and I imagined that he had indeed liked the meat. I had no idea that the gardener's wife had thrashed him and chased him out of the compound, and would not let him enter even the garden, and that is why he spent time sitting by the wayside in front of the gate. My servants were also complicit in this arrangement.

Suddenly, I fell ill again, and could not come down for around two days. That afternoon, I was lying on my bed, and I had just finished reading the newspaper. I was gazing through the window at the hot afternoon sky absentmindedly, and thinking about the Congress leaders' aggressive desire to become ministers. Yet they used such stratagems to hide this—mask it under the cloak of indifference. The state power would not listen to a word of what they had demanded, and passed laws completely disregarding them. Yet, they would still analyse these laws and fight with the government as to why the laws were bad! They desired to prove to everyone that the government's intentions were not good. What a dilemma!

Suddenly, through the door the shadow of a dog could be seen. I looked round to see my guest standing there wagging his tail. In the afternoon the servants were all asleep, their rooms shut, and using this chance, he had slunk right in front of my door. I thought, he had not seen me for two days and that is why he must have come to visit me. So I called out, 'Come in, my guest, come into the room.' He would not come in, but simply stood near the door wagging his tail. I asked him, 'Have you eaten? What did they give you to eat?' I suddenly felt that his eyes were a little wet, that he had come secretly to complain to me. As I called the servants, and their doors opened, the guest ran away. I asked them, 'Hey, did you give the dog food today?'

They said, 'No babu. The gardener's wife drove him away.'

I enquired, 'But today there was quite a lot of leftovers? What happened to that?'

'The gardener's wife has taken it all.'

My friend woke up at the disturbance, and came into the room rubbing his eyes and smiling slightly, said, 'Dada can really create situations. Human beings cannot eat, but he invites street dogs and gives them food. Nice!' My friend knew that this logic was irrefutable. Giving food to dogs instead of giving it to human beings! Hearing it, I kept silent. How could I explain to them that in this world, claims of someone on somebody else did not operate according to strict rules.

However that was, my guest was called back, and he again took his place, unperturbed, in the dust under the portico. He even lost his fear of the gardener's wife. When the day was over, and late afternoon came around, I saw from the first floor verandah that my guest was looking my way expectantly. It was time to go for a walk.

I did not get better, but my time to leave Deoghar came by. I tried to delay it by two to three days using various excuses. But since this morning, packing has begun—the train is in the afternoon. Outside the gate, a line of vehicles are waiting, and our things begin to be loaded on these. Today, my guest is very busy, for he has taken onto himself the task of supervision—nothing should get lost in the melee—and so he is running about with great energy, his enthusiasm is greater than anybody else's.

One by one the vehicles move forward, and even mine begins to roll onwards. The station is not far off, and we reach it soon. When I begin to get down I see that my guest is standing there. I ask, 'You have come here as well?' He wags his tail in response; I do not know what it means!

Tickets are bought, the luggage is loaded into the train, and my friend comes and informs me that the train is leaving in another minute. All who had come to see us off get tips—only my guest does not get anything. The dust stirred up by the hot air has obscured the far-off view. Before I leave, I see through the haze the dim silhouette of my guest standing near the gate of the station—he is watching intently. As the train leaves, I do not find a drop of excitement in my heart at the prospect of returning home. I keep thinking that today my guest will go back to the house to find the iron gates closed; there would be no way of entering. He will wait on the road for a day or two, he will perhaps sneak in some quiet afternoon and look for me in my room upstairs, and then, a street dog will take shelter on the street again.

Perhaps, there is not a single living being more insignificant than he is, and yet it is only with him in mind that I leave behind, in writing, the memories of my few days' stay at Deoghar.

eight

HARICHARAN*

*T*his had happened many years ago. More than ten to twelve years. Durgadas-babu had not turned into a lawyer—as early as that. You might not know Durgadas Bandopadhyay, but I know him quite well. Come, let me make him known to you.

While still a child, an orphaned young boy—one doesn't know wherefrom—from a Kayastha family, had sought shelter under Ramdas-babu's wing, and was granted a safe haven. Everyone used to comment, 'The boy is indeed a gem!' He was a good looking and intelligent boy, and soon grew to be a very dear servant to Durgadas-babu's father.

He used to be very eager to perform every little task himself. From giving the cow her feed, to giving the babu an oil massage, he chased every task to the end. He loved to be busy all the time.

His name was Haricharan. The mistress would constantly get surprised at Haricharan's ever-present desire to serve.

---

*Translated from the original with the same title, in *SSS*, Vol. 2, pp. 1698–99.

Sometimes, she would even chide him fondly and say, 'Hari, there are other servants too. You are a child; why do you have to work so hard?' If Hari had a fault, it was that he loved to smile. So he would smile and reply, 'Maa, we are poor people, and anyway we have to work our whole life. What is the point of just sitting and doing nothing?'

In such a manner, amidst work, in contentment, and surrounded by love and affection, a year went by.

Suro was Ramdas-babu's youngest daughter. Suro was about five to six years of age and she shared a deep sense of kinship with Haricharan. When Suro would rebel against drinking milk, and engage in battle with her mother, the mother, even despite much unnecessary arguments, could not compel her tiny daughter to have the milk. Anxious about her daughter's health, her mind would leap to her precious daughter's inevitable demise without milk, and she would become thoroughly enraged. She would lock her fingers hard on Surobala's cheeks to prise her mouth open but still fail to feed her milk—then, Haricharan's interventions would prove fruitful.

Indeed, I have carried on pointlessly for far too long. Let me come to the hub of the matter now, do listen. Perhaps Suro loved Haricharan.

I will talk about the time when Durgadas-babu was just twenty years old. Durgadas had so far remained in Calcutta for his education. To come home he would have to first travel south by steamer, then walk through some ten to twelve krosh on foot. As it was not a very easy journey, Durgadas-babu did not come home very often.

Now the son had finally completed his BA and had returned home. His mother was very busy. The boy would have to be fed, would have to be pampered—the whole household was on its toes to cater to his every need.

Durgadas asked, 'Maa, who is this boy?' His mother answered, 'He is the son of a Kayeth[1]; he has no parents, so the master has kept him for himself. He performs all the tasks of a servant, and he is very quiet. He does not get angry at anything. Ahaa![2] He has no parents; on top of that, he is a child—I love him very much.'

When Durgadas-babu came home, this is what he learnt about Haricharan.

That may be so, but nowadays Haricharan's workload has increased enormously. He is not unhappy about it; no, indeed, he is very happy about it. Chhotobabu[3] did not just need help while bathing, but Haricharan also proved to be very deft at keeping a pot of water handy for certain necessities, a box of betel leaves at the right time, and the hubble-bubble was always ready for use during leisure hours. Durgadas-babu even got into the way of thinking that the boy was quite intelligent, and therefore, if Haricharan did not pleat his dhotis, or prepare his hubble-bubble, Durgadas-babu did not feel satisfied.

But flowing water has such strange pathways, no matter where its origins are. Have you experienced it? From good it is not always necessary that only good will emerge; sometimes even evil emerges. If you have never noticed such strange outcomes, come, I will draw your attention to such unfathomable matters.

---

[1]Kayeth or Kayastha
[2]'Ahaa' is an expression of well-meant and deeply felt empathy, here, at the plight of the orphan Haricharan.
[3]'Chhotobabu' here is Durgadas-babu.

The few words set out above will remain opaque to many, and, anyway, it is not necessary to understand it right away. I too have no desire to get into philosophical discussions; between you and me, I am just filling in the background. No harm in that, is there?

Today, Durgadas-babu has been invited to a grand dinner. He will not dine at home, and very possibly he will return home very late. For these reasons he has told Haricharan to finish his daily chores and go to bed.

Now let me come to Haricharan. Durgadas-babu used to sleep in the drawing room at night. Many do not know the reason for this. I think he preferred to sleep in the drawing room because his wife was at her parents' house.

It was Haricharan's duty to make Durgadas-babu's bed, and when his master prepared for sleep, to press his feet. When Durgadas-babu would go off to sleep, Haricharan would retire to bed in the next room.

From early evening that day, Haricharan's head began to ache. He understood that he was in for a bout of fever, for he occasionally suffered from these attacks. He was familiar with all the signs. As he could not remain upright, he went to his room and lay down. He did not remember that Chhotobabu's bed remained unmade. At night, everyone had their meals but Haricharan did not turn up. The mistress came to see for herself, and found Haricharan sleeping. She touched him and observed that he was burning up. Realizing he had a fever, she quietly left without disturbing him.

The night had now rolled on to 2 a.m. Durgadas-babu finished his dinner, and came home to find that his bed was not ready. Not only was he sleepy, but on his way back home he had been pleasantly anticipating how he would return to lie in his bed while Haricharan would take off his shoes and press his feet, and he would sleepily welcome the morning with his hubble-bubble in hand.

Extremely disappointed, his temper flared up. He yelled 'Horey, Horey'[4] a couple of times, but where was Hari? He was lying almost unconscious with fever. At this lack of response, Durgadas-babu thought, 'The fellow must have gone to sleep'. He peeped into the next room, and saw him rolled up in a sheet.

He could not tolerate it any more. With tremendous force, he tried to pull Hari up by his hair, but Hari flopped right back onto the bed. Then Durgadas-babu lost all control over his senses in rage and kicked Hari in the back with his boot-shod feet. At such a heavy thrashing, Hari regained his consciousness and sat up. Durgadas-babu savagely taunted, 'Little baby has fallen asleep … Will I make my own bed?' His temper rose again, and the cane in his hand landed a few more times on Hari's back.

When that night Hari was pressing his feet, perhaps a drop of warm tear fell on Durgadas-babu's foot.

Durgadas-babu could not sleep the remainder of the night. The drop of tear had felt very hot. Durgadas-babu was very fond of Haricharan. He was not only Durgadas-babu's favourite, but everyone loved him because of his gentle nature. Especially, owing to the affectionate relationship that had come to grow between the two of them for over a month, Hari had become even more dear to him.

That night, many times, Durgadas-babu was on the brink of going and checking for himself how much Hari had been hurt, and whether the weals left by the cane had swollen over

---

[4]A short, irate form of 'Haricharan'.

much. But Hari was a servant, it would be so embarrassing. Many times he thought of going and asking if his fever had abated somewhat. But again he felt ashamed of doing so! In the morning, Haricharan brought water for his morning ablutions, and prepared his hubble-bubble. Even then, if Durgadas-babu had expressed some sympathy, had said, 'Ahaa!' He was just a child, he had not yet crossed thirteen; if he had pulled him close, like he would a child, and seen for himself how raw the weals raised by the whipping were, how swollen the bruises from the edges of his boots were! Why feel embarrassed before a boy!

At nine in the morning, a telegram arrived for him. Durgadas-babu's heart gave a jump of fear. He opened it and saw that his wife was very ill. His heart sank to his shoes. He had to leave for Calcutta that very day. As he climbed into the carriage, he thought, 'God, maybe it is time for repentance.'

◆

A month has gone by. Today, Durgadas-babu wears a very cheerful face. His wife has pulled through this time, and has been given her first solid meal.

Today, a letter has arrived from home. Durgadas-babu's youngest brother had written it. Right at the very bottom, after a 'postscript' is written—'It is very sad, yesterday morning, after suffering from a high fever for ten days, our Haricharan has died. Before dying he had wanted to see you many times.'

Ahaa! The poor motherless, fatherless orphan!

Very slowly, Durgadas-babu tore the letter into a hundred pieces.

nine

BILASI[*][1]

I walk over two krosh of village pathways to acquire education in a school. Not just me alone—there are some ten to twelve of us. Eighty per cent children of all the families who stay in a village have to acquire education in this manner. Even if the education that was acquired with such difficulty amounted to something, a guess as to its net profit can be made if a few simple equations are considered. The boys have to leave the house at 8 a.m., and have to walk a total of four krosh. Four krosh does not mean merely eight miles—it is actually much more. During the monsoons, the boys walk knee-deep in mud with the rain pelting down, and in summer, under the harsh sun, and instead of mud, they have to swim to school through oceans of dust. One wonders whether the Goddess Saraswati, pleased at the hardship these unfortunate boys undergo, grants

---

*Copied from the diary of a village boy. There is no need for anyone to know his real name. His pet name—say—is Nyadaa.

[1]Translated from the original with the same title 'Bilasi', in *SSS*, Vol. 2, pp. 1707–13.

them boons, or horrified at such suffering, averts her face.

When these children finish their schooling, they either settle in the village or go away where there is a livelihood—but the four krosh-long walk every day to acquire education, builds such reserves of inner power, that inevitably there are outward manifestations. I have heard some people comment, 'Well, even if you count out the poor, there are families without economic hardships. Why do they run away from the villages? If they were to remain, the villages would not reflect such abysmal poverty.'

I will not lug the issue of malaria into this. But the prospect of those four krosh of compulsory walking have forced countless number of bhadralok along with their children into towns. When the children's education is finally over, they get so used to the conveniences of living in towns, it no longer seems feasible to return to the village.

Let such pointless discussions rest. We go to school. We have to trudge through two or three villages on the way. We get ample opportunity to find out important facts. Like mangoes ripening in A's orchard; in which forest there are countless bunches of *boinchi* fruit waiting to be picked; jackfruits on such and such a person's tree are beginning to ripen; a bunch of *martaman* bananas[2] in B's banana grove is just waiting to be cut; C's pineapple bush is sporting pineapples that are turning a lovely colour; from D's palm tree growing near his water tank one can eat dates with the minimal danger of being caught—we spend much time on acquiring these interesting bits of information. But we do not find much time for what should count as actual knowledge, like what

---

[2] A variety of banana.

the capital of Kamchatka[3] is, and whether gold or silver was mined in the Siberian mines.

During examinations, we would put down Aden as a Persian port, and Humayun's father's name as Tughlaq Khan. I find that even though I have turned forty, my grasp of these subjects have remained more or less at that level. We would all gather with glum faces when the results for promotion would be announced, and plan to beat up the teacher, or decide it was our duty to leave such a bad school.

Now and then I used to meet a boy from our village on my way to school. His name was Mrityunjoy. He was much older than us. He used to study in the third class. When he was first promoted to the third class, none of us knew—possibly it was an archaeologist's topic of research—but we have always known him to study in the third class.

We have never heard of him studying in the fourth class, or if he had ever been in the second class. He did not have either parents or brothers and sisters. He had only a huge orchard full of mangoes and jackfruit trees, and a tumble-down house inside it; he also had an uncle. It was the uncle's profession to spread dark tales about his nephew—that he smoked ganja, that he took opium balls, and things of a similar nature. He was also fond of spreading around his claim to half of the orchard—he was just waiting to put in a legal claim, and then he would take possession of his share. He, of course, did get possession of it but not through the order of the district court, but through the order of a far higher court up there. But we will come to that later.

---

[3]Kamchatka peninsular is located in far-eastern Russia and known for its wildlife, volcanoes, etc.

Mrityunjoy used to cook for himself. During the mango season, he would lease out the orchard and based on the proceeds, his expenses for the entire year used to be met, and met very well. Whenever we saw him, he would be walking silently with his torn and worn out books tucked under his arm. We have never seen him ever come forward on his own to talk to us. On the contrary, we would take the initiative to talk to him. The main reason for this was that there was no one like him in the village—so ready to stand us treats in the village eateries. And not just boys. I have lost count of the number of fathers who would put up their sons to ask him to disburse money upon the flimsiest of excuses—the loss of money set aside for school fees, stolen books, et cetera, et cetera. But forget about acknowledging such debts, the fathers were reluctant to socially acknowledge that their sons were in the habit of speaking to him. Such was the wonderful reputation Mrityunjoy enjoyed in the village.

We did not see Mrityunjoy for many days. Then one day we heard he was almost dying. Then again we heard that an old Mal[4] from Malpada was his physician and his daughter, Bilasi, had nursed him back from the maws of Yamraj,[5] and had saved him this time round.

My heart ached a bit—after all, I had wolfed down the sweets which he used to buy for me. One evening, I surreptitiously went to meet him. Around his house, there was no wall to speak of. I walked in easily, and found the door to the room open. A lamp was burning brightly within and Mrityunjoy was lying on a spotlessly white bed on a wooden

---

[4]Mal is a low-caste community of snake charmers.
[5]The God of Death in Hinduism.

cot. A mere glance at his skeletal frame was enough to confirm that Yamraj had indeed tried very hard, but at long last, had had to retreat—defeated—before the intense fight this girl had put up against him. She was sitting at the head of the bed and fanning him. She gave a start when, suddenly, she spotted a stranger entering the room, and then stood up. So this was the snake charmer's daughter, Bilasi. I could not tell whether she was eighteen or twenty-eight. But the instant I glanced at her face, I knew past all doubt that no matter what her age, under the tremendous pressure of nursing Mrityunjoy round the clock and keeping sleepless vigils over the patient, there was nothing left of her. Just like stale flowers wet with water in a vase. If one would only slightly touch them, move them a little, they would shed all their petals.

Mrityunjoy recognized me and asked, 'Who is it—Nyadaa?'

I said, 'Hmm.'

Mrityunjoy said, 'Sit down.'

The girl remained standing with her head bent. Mrityunjoy, in a few words, explained that he had been ill for a month and a half, within which duration he had remained senseless and comatose for a fortnight. It was only over the last few days that he had begun to recognize people and even though he could not as yet leave his bed, there was nothing to fear any more.

Maybe the crisis was over. But young as I was, I could at least understand that the responsibility of undertaking the nursing of someone who even today was unable to leave his bed, must be indeed very onerous. Day after day, night after night, such kindness, such constant care, so many sleepless nights! Such a courageous act! Even though that day I did not understand the secret source of such strength, I did become acquainted with it at a later date.

When I was ready to return, the girl brought another lamp and accompanied me right up to the broken wall. Till now, she had not spoken a word, but now she asked gently, 'Shall I take you up to the main road?'

Owing to the big mango trees, the orchard appeared like a wall of thick darkness—one could not see the palm of one's hand. I said, 'There is no need to come with me, just give me the lamp.'

When she handed me the lamp, I caught a glimpse of her anxious face. She again asked gently, 'You will not feel scared to go on your own? Shall I come with you a little way?'

A girl was asking me if I would feel afraid! Whatever might be my state of mind, I had to reply briefly, 'No', and then step forward.

She warned, 'The path is through a heavy forest, be careful where you place your foot.'

I felt goosebumps rise on my skin, for I finally knew why she was anxious and why she had wanted to escort me through the jungle with a lamp. Perhaps she would not have listened to my protests and would have come with me regardless, but for the fact that the ill Mrityunjoy would be left on his own.

The orchard was a good twenty to twenty-five *bigha*s. The road was not short. Perhaps I would have been scared at every footstep in this heavy darkness, had not my thoughts about that girl so completely absorbed me that I had no time to feel scared. I thought, it must have been so difficult to be constantly with a patient hovering between life and death. Mrityunjoy could have died any moment; then what would the girl have done all alone at night, in this deep forest? How would she have spent the night with no one around?

In this context, another incident—which had occurred much later in my life—came to me. I was present at the deathbed of a relative. It was a dark night, there were no servants or children at home—just the recently widowed woman and I. His wife, in the throes of a wild grief, was so unrestrained in her lamentations that I began to fear that such paroxysms would carry her off too. She constantly cried and through her tears repeatedly asked me, why would the government be concerned if she willingly mounted the funeral pyre of her husband? Would they not understand that she had no desire to live another moment? Did they not have wives? Were they made of stone? And if this very night, some people from the village made suitable arrangements in some jungle next to the river, how would the police know anyway? And much more in this strain. I, however, could not afford to just sit there and listen to her wails. I had to inform the neighbourhood; I had to make arrangements for the cremation too. However, the moment she heard of my resolve to leave the house, she normalized. She wiped her eyes, and said, 'Bhai, whatever had to happen has happened. What's the point in going out now? Let the night pass.'

I said, 'There is a lot of work to be done, I must go.'

She returned, 'Let there be work. You sit here.'

I patiently answered, 'I cannot just sit here, I have to inform everybody,' but the moment I attempted to take a step forward, she screamed, '*Orey baprey*! I cannot stay on my own.'

And so I had to sit down again. For I realized that she might have lived fearlessly with a husband who was alive for upwards of twenty-five years, but even if she managed to face his death, she could not face his dead body for even five minutes alone, at night. If anything could kill her it would be a little while spent next to her husband's dead body all by herself.

But it is not my intention to portray her grief as trivial. Nor is it my desire to even insinuate that it was not genuine. Nor do I want to say that the matter is resolved by this one example. I know many other incidents: even without bringing them into this discussion, I just want to observe that no woman can overcome this fear simply out of a sense of duty or just because they have lived with the husband for years on end. Only that one power can set aside that fear—a power that a husband and wife who have merely lived together for even a hundred years, might not be able to fathom.

But if one spots that power in any man–woman relationship, and even though social norms may condemn their union, a sense of universal humanity will compel a person to shed tears discreetly.

For almost two months, I did not enquire after Mrityunjoy's health. Those who have not seen a village, or have just seen it through the windows of a train, might now exclaim in amazement, 'Is such a thing possible! You did not enquire after his health even though you saw with your own eyes how very ill he had been!' I must say for their information, that not only is it possible, but this is what happens. I know there is a popular conception that in village societies the moment someone is in trouble, the entire community turns up in force to succour him. Whether such mentalities existed in the villages of the *Satyayuga*[6] I cannot say, but in this day and age

---

[6]The first phase of the four cycles of time in Hindu religious philosophy—Satya, Dwapar, Treta and Kali.

I have never seen such a thing happen in my memory. Still, I can say with certainty that since there was no news of his death, he must be alive.

Suddenly, one day we heard that Mrityunjoy's uncle with a claim to Mrityunjoy's orchard was agitating around the village and beating his breast about the imminent and inevitable destruction of the village, that he would be unable to show his face in the society as the Mitra of Nalter—the useless fellow had brought home the daughter of a snake charmer after nikaah. Not just nikaah, which could still be set aside, but had actually accepted cooked rice from her hands! If the village did not punish such insolent disregard for religious prescriptions, then people may as well live in forests. If any of this had happened in the societies of Kodola or in Haripur, it would have…et cetera, et cetera.

Then, only one expression of horror ensued from the lips of everyone—from old men to young boys—'Ahaha! What is happening! Is Kali[7] all set to overturn all rules?'

The uncle set out with enhanced enthusiasm around the village and began to say that he had had a prescience of such a thing happening. He had just been watching the fun, waiting to see where it would all end. Otherwise, was Mrityunjoy not his own nephew, could he not have taken him to his own residence and taken care of his nephew's medical treatment himself? Did he not have the wherewithal to command the services of doctors? Now let everyone witness why he had not done so! But now, it was impossible to remain silent! For now the name of the Mitra lineage was getting

---

[7]Kaliyuga is the last phase of the time cycle in Hindu philosophy, when all human virtues and order are corrupted.

blackened! The village itself was burning up under such insolent defiance!

Then we, the villagers, did something in concert, for which, even today, I burn with shame when it comes to mind. The uncle marched to protect the revered name of the Mitra lineage, and ten to twelve of us marched with him to stop the village from languishing under insolence.

When we reached Mrityunjoy's tumble-down house, it was just getting to be evening. The girl was rolling rotis on one side of the broken verandah. She turned blue with terror when suddenly she saw a large number of people armed with heavy sticks.

The uncle peeped into the room and saw Mrityunjoy lying on the cot. He quickly chained the door from the outside and started to address the girl in terms that perhaps no uncle in the whole world had ever used to address his nephew's wife. They were such that even a girl from a low-down snake charmer's caste raised her eyes and said, 'Do you know that my father has married me to him!'

The uncle roared, 'How dare you?' and followed it up by more of the same. Right away, some ten to twelve of us bravely leaped on her, one caught hold of her hair, another her ears, yet another her hands—and those who did not manage to get hold of anything, also did not remain passive assaulters.

Even Lord Narayan's superiors will feel embarrassment to spread a black lie[8]—that we maintain a cowardly mien in the battlefield—when there is no doubt about our prowess in tough combat.

---

[8]An irreverent and satirical expression signifying that even gods could not malign the Bengali's courage.

Let me say something quite irrelevant here. I have heard that in the mlecchha[9] Western countries there is a superstitious irrationality that forbids men to raise their hands against women because they are weak and helpless. On the contrary, we say that hands should be raised only on those who are helpless—whoever that might be—woman or man.

The girl had just screamed once at the beginning, and then she had gone completely silent. But when we began to drag her out of the village, she began to plead, 'Please babu, just let me go once, let me leave the rotis inside the room. Otherwise dogs and jackals will eat them up—the poor invalid will not be able to eat the whole night.'

Mrityunjoy was beating his head against the locked door, kicking it, and mouthing both pleas and abuses in varied and colourful language. But we did not get even slightly upset by such irrelevant emotions. For the welfare of the country we bore all unflinchingly and continued to drag her pitilessly out of the village.

I say 'we', but for some weakness that was still in me, I had not been able to hit her. Instead, I felt like crying. She had committed a serious crime, and it was indeed mete that she should be turned out of the village, but I just could not think that our own actions were right. But, no doubt, my reflections have no importance.

You must not think that we, in the village, are not capable of generosity. Not at all. Indeed, if there are important and rich people, you would be surprised to know how generous we can be.

If even Mrityunjoy had not taken rice from her hands and

---

[9]Communities outside the Brahminic sociopolitical and ritualistic hierarchy.

thus committed such an unpardonable crime, we would not have been so annoyed. The nikaah of a Kayastha's son with a snake charmer's daughter was nothing but a laughable matter! But the ingestion of cooked rice had been fatal for Mrityunjoy. It was immaterial that he had been ill for over two-and-a-half months, and that he was bedridden. But rice—not *luchis*[10], not meat, not sweets! Eating cooked rice was a sin against food! Truly it could not be forgiven. Otherwise the people of the villages are not at all narrow-minded. The same boys who painfully acquire knowledge after a daily four krosh-trudge, one day acquire the status of leaders of the society. They have been blessed by Goddess Binapani[11] herself—how can their minds be afflicted with narrowness?

A few days after this incident, the widowed daughter-in-law of the departed and most holy Mukhopadhyay Mohashoyey, returned from her two-year-long residence in Kashi, a haven sought out of sheer heartbreak. Whispers began to fly amongst the gossipmongers that Chhotobabu (the widow's younger brother-in-law) had persuaded her to return from a place that was—of course Kashi—and indeed he had expended huge amounts of effort to do so solely because the widow owned half the property and he did not want to lose it. Whatever might be the case, Chhotobabu, out of pure generosity, donated two hundred rupees for the yearly Durga puja. He also invited the Brahmins of the five surrounding villages and put before them a fine meal, besides a bell-metal glass in every departing Brahmin's hand; his praise began to be sung all over. The replete invitees, on their way home, loudly proclaimed that

---

[10]Deep-fried, flat breads made out of wheat flour.
[11]Goddess Saraswati

the country and countrymen would both benefit equally if all the similarly wealthy households arranged for such functions every month.

Never mind. We have many such tales of glory. They have accumulated through the centuries, and have piled up before almost every villager's doorstep. I have travelled across many such villages in South Bengal, and I have witnessed much that would justifiably make us proud. Our education is totally complete—whether you consider the question of our strength of character, or of religion, or of knowledge. Now it is only a matter of abusing the English soundly—the country will then certainly achieve independence.

A year has gone by. Being absolutely unable to withstand the attacks of the mosquitoes, I have just returned home after resigning my position of a sannyasi. One afternoon, as I was walking through Malpada, I suddenly recognized Mrityunjoy sitting before the door of a hut. He had a saffron-coloured turban on his head, long hair and beard, strings of beads and *rudraksha* around his neck—who would have recognized him ever as the Mrityunjoy we all once knew. A son of a Kayastha had, in one year, given up his caste and had completely transformed into a snake charmer. It is indeed strange how quickly a man might give up his social identity handed down to him over fourteen generations, and metamorphose into something else. I am sure you have all heard of the Brahmin boy who had married a sweeper and had picked up the caste occupation of a sweeper. I have seen the son of a good Brahmin family marry a Dom girl and himself become a Dom, even though he had passed the Entrance Examination[12]. Now he

---

[12] A public examination introduced by the colonial educational system.

sells cane sieves and looks after herds of swine. I have even seen a boy from a Kayastha family marry a butcher's daughter and transform into a full-fledged butcher. Today, he slaughters cows with his own hands and sells the meat—just looking at him, nobody will believe that he was anything else ever at any point in time. But the reason lying behind all these complete metamorphoses is the same. I, therefore, sometimes think that, cannot those who can pull down a man so easily, push them up as easily? Are all the praises that I have sung about the men in the Bengal villages solely reserved for them? Are they powered in their swift downhill journey by their own steam? Is there not even a little encouragement, even a little help from the inside of the household?

Let it be. I do not want to get into arguments about matters that are no concern of mine. Yet, the dilemma is that I just cannot forget the fact that ninety per cent of our people live in villages, and therefore we have to do something about it. Never mind. As I was saying, it was difficult to believe this was Mrityunjoy. However, he bade me welcome affectionately. Bilasi had gone to fetch water. When she saw me she too expressed great happiness. She repeatedly said, 'If you had not intervened that night, those villagers would have surely murdered me. They must have beaten you too.'

I learnt through our conversation, that the next day the two had escaped to Malpada, and they had gradually built their home up, and were now living happily. They did not have to tell me they were happy, I could gather as much from their faces.

The moment I heard that they were on the point of leaving as they had been hired for catching a snake in some village, I jumped with joy. One of the two of my dearest wishes ever since childhood, was to keep—as pets—cobras and *gokhuras*[13]. The other was to command the forces of nature with spells (*mantrasiddhva*).

So far, I hadn't found a way of becoming a *siddhva*[14], but now that I had found Mrityunjoy, I felt joyously sure he would become my ustad. His father-in-law was well-known, and Mrityunjoy, as his disciple, was a great man. That my fate would come to smile upon me so fortuitously, nobody could have foreseen.

Both were very reluctant at first, for the work was both dangerous and difficult. However, I was so insistent that within a month Mrityunjoy had capitulated and enrolled me as his disciple. He taught me the spells and the calculations required for catching snakes. He also tied to my wrist amulets containing medicines, and turned me into a full-fledged snake charmer. Do you want to know the spell? I remember the last stanza went like this:

> *Orey Cobra, you are the bearer of Manasa*[15]
> *Manasa devi is my mother—*
> *Pierce the lower regions—turn rules topsy turvy.*
> *Take the poison of the dhoda*[16], *give your poison to the dhoda.*
> *Oh Dudhraj*[17], *Moniraj*[18]!
> *By whose command—by Vishari's*[19] *command.*

---

[13]A highly venomous snake seen in many regions of the Indian subcontinent.
[14]A person who has acquired power through yogic meditations.
[15]The goddess of snakes.
[16]A non-venomous snake.
[17]The king of snakes fond of drinking milk.
[18]The king of snakes with a jewel in his head.
[19]The goddess of snakes who, if inclined to be kind, can extract poison from fatally-bitten victims.

I do not know what these lines mean: the reason being I have never set eyes on the *rishi*—there surely had to be one who had created these lines.

Of course one day the final judgement was pronounced on whether these lines were true or false, but much before then, I attained a huge reputation all over the region as a snake-catcher. Everyone was in agreement, 'Yes, Nyadaa has become a talented man indeed! He had gone to Kamakhya as a sannyasi and has come back as a siddhva.' I became so conceited at the thought of being considered a great ustad at such a young age, that those days my feet did not touch the ground.

Only two people did not believe in it. My guru, characteristically, never uttered either a word of praise or of blame. But Bilasi would occasionally say with a slight smirk, 'Thakur, these are all very dangerous animals, please be a little careful when you handle them.' Indeed, I had started treating jobs like breaking the poison ducts, or extracting poison out of the snakes' mouths, so carelessly that today, when I think back, I still get the shivers.

The truth is this, that snake-catching is not very difficult, and after a snake has been confined in a pot for a couple of days, whether the poison ducts are broken or not, it loses the desire to strike. It just raises its hood pretending to bite, gives one the scares, but does not bite.

Occasionally, Bilasi would argue with the pair of us—guru and disciple. The most profitable business of the snake charmers was the sale of roots and herbs, the very display of which would compel the snakes to leave. But before that, there was a small task that had to be done—a heated iron rod would be touched to its mouth a couple of times, and after that whether it was shown the right root or a harmless twig, it would certainly depart. Bilasi was dead against this practice, and would strongly protest when Mrityunjoy displayed no qualms about it: 'Look, do not cheat people like this.'

Mrityunjoy would defend himself, 'Why not? Everyone does it. Where is the harm in it?'

Bilasi would retort, 'Let them. We don't have any trouble getting square meals, why should we cheat people unnecessarily?'

I have noticed something else that happened regularly. Whenever we received a call for catching snakes, Bilasi would try her level best to stop us—she would trot out the excuse of a Tuesday, or Saturday or something else. If Mrityunjoy was not present, she used to chase them away immediately, but when he was present, Mrityunjoy could not resist the lure of quick money. As for me, catching snakes had become like a heady addiction. I did not, therefore hesitate to get him all excited. Indeed, there was no space for fear in what seemed to me to be total fun. But one day I had to bear the punishment for my sin.

That day we had gone to a cowherd's house to catch a snake. Bilasi was with us, for she always accompanied us on these trips. We had just dug a little into the mud floor, when the signs of a hole became visible. None of us had noticed but Bilasi was a daughter of a snake charmer and she bent to pick up a few bits of paper. She warned me, 'Thakur, be careful when you dig. There is at least a pair of snakes here, if not more. Certainly not just one.'

Mrityunjoy said, 'But these people said, that only one has come in. They have just seen one.'

Bilasi showed the paper and said, 'Cannot you see they had built a nest?'

Mrityunjoy said, 'But even mice can bring paper.'

Bilasi said, 'Both are possibilities. But I am certain there are at least two.'

In truth, Bilasi's prognosis was absolutely correct, and was confirmed by a heart-rending tragedy. Within ten minutes, Mrityunjoy caught a huge kharish gokhura and gave it to me. I had barely turned after putting it in the basket when Mrityunjoy let out a gasp of pain, breathed a sigh and came out (of the room). The back of his hand was bleeding heavily.

We were rendered witless for a moment. That in the act of catching a snake it would, instead of being desperate to escape, shoot out a long neck from the burrow and strike—I have witnessed such an unthinkable situation like this only once in life. The next instant, Bilasi screamed, ran forward and tightly bound his hand with her sari-end. She also gave him to chew all the roots and herbs she had brought with her. I took off my amulet, and tied it along with Mrityunjoy's own amulet. We hoped that this would prevent the poison from rising up the blood stream. I also started to chant repeatedly that spell about the *Vishari* with great energy. A crowd gathered around, and people ran hither and thither to get as many medicinal experts from around the area as they could find. Someone ran to give Bilasi's father the news as well.

I was not sparing myself in the chanting of the spell, but I could not help feeling it was not helping much. Nevertheless, I did not slacken my efforts. However, after about fifteen to twenty minutes, when Mrityunjoy vomited once and then started talking through his nose, Bilasi flung herself down upon the ground. I also figured out, perhaps my appeals to *Vishari* were not working satisfactorily.

A few more ustads from the nearby neighbourhoods turned up, and all of us began to address the thirty-three crore gods and goddesses sometimes individually, sometimes collectively. But the poison refused to be addressed. The patient's condition began to deteriorate. When it was clear that gentle pleas would not be effective, three or four shamans began to abuse the poison so violently that if the poison possessed ears, it would have left the region in fright, not just Mrityunjoy. But nothing helped. After another half an hour of struggle, Mrityunjoy proved false the name of Mritunjyoy given by his parents, his father-in-law's spells and medicines, and departed from this world. Bilasi was sitting with her husband's head on her lap, she sat as if turned to stone.

No, I will not expand on her sad story. I will end the story by saying that she had just managed to live another seven days. She only once told me, 'Thakur, I am making you swear on me, the binding of *dibbi*[20], you will never do all this again.'

My amulets and medicines had all accompanied Mrityunjoy to his grave, only the command of *Vishari* still remained. But even I had managed to comprehend that her command was nowhere similar to the command of the magistrate, and that snake's poison was not the poison of the average Bengali.

One day, when I went to visit her, I heard that she had committed suicide—there was no dearth of snake's poison in the house; she had swallowed some. According to the shastras, she must have gone to hell. But wherever she may have gone, I can only say that when my time comes I will not step back from going there.

---

[20]A vow taken by a sacred swearing which has the power to bind the person it is cast on.

The uncle got possession of the entire orchard and like a learned person, began to trot around the village saying, 'If he will not die an accidental death, who will? A man might have ten such relationships, not just one, and at the most there will be a little gossip. But why did he have to take cooked rice—that was what killed him! He has died, and he has also lowered my head in shame. Neither did he get a little fire, nor any offering of *pindi*[21], or any consecrated meals (in *shraddh*s).'

The villagers also agreed unanimously, 'Where is any doubt about that? Sin against food![22] *Baap rey!* Is there any penance for that!'

Even the matter of Bilasi's suicide became a subject of mockery to many. I often think, maybe both of them had committed the crime of suicide. Still, Mrityunjoy was a child of the village, he had grown up in that environment. Did no one ever try to see what power it was that had driven him to such a recklessly brave act?

I think, that in a country where there is no established norm for a man and a woman to win each other's hearts first before marriage, but contrarily it is an object of condemnation; in a country whose men and women are deprived of the good fortune to hope, or the terrible joy of desire; who don't, even for once, have to carry the pride of victory and the agony at defeat; in such a country this power will never be visible. There are no individualistic qualms about making

---

[21]The first offering of cooked rice to the dead. Funereal rites are called *shraddh*s.

[22]The uncle ascribed a terrible end to a sin (*paap*) against the sacred dharma or duty of maintaining caste purity which was not lost by illicit sexual intercourse but through accepting cooked rice (*onno*): this amounted to 'onno-paap'/anna/annam from the hands of impure castes.

personal choices or making mistakes or suffering through flat refusals. Likewise, there is no individualistic complacence at not having made mistakes. The old and venerable traditions of a very wise society have carefully separated the people from all sorts of imbroglios, and have provided a clear way of always maintaining a 'good' life forever. Thus, to those for whom marriage means a simple contract—whether made permanent with Vedic bonds or not—Mrityunjoy's reason for committing the ultimate sin against food would be indeed unfathomable. Those who mocked Bilasi's suicide, are all either sadhu householders or *saddhvi*[23] wives—and I am certain they will all achieve *akshay sati-lok*[24]. But when that snake charmer's daughter had gradually won the heart of a bedridden invalid, I am sure not one of these respectable persons have ever felt even a fraction of the proud joy she had experienced then. Mrityunjoy was a very ordinary person, but the joy of winning his heart is not an ordinary thing and neither is possessing that treasure negligible.

It is this power of love that is difficult for the people of this country to understand. I will not criticize Bhudev-babu's[25] essay on familial ties, nor will I criticize the social norms and regulations expressed therein. Even if I do, there will be many who will answer harshly, 'On the basis of such norms and regulations, the Hindu social structure has survived countless centuries of revolutions and changes.' I respect these learned body of scholars very deeply, and I will not say in reply that

---

[23]The female equivalent of the *sadhu*, or ascetic.

[24]*Akshay* can be understood as eternal, while *sati-lok* is the eternal heaven for virtuous wives.

[25]Bhudev Mukhopadhyay was a nineteenth-century intellectual, who wrote on modern education, modern times and modern customs.

'survival is not the most important realization in life—the mammoth has perished but the cockroach has survived'. I will only say, that while there is no doubt that the chubby baby of the wealthy, always carried around and constantly watched, will remain pretty good, possibly, however, instead of preserving it carefully in exactly the same form as the cockroach, if he is set down on the ground now and then, and like everybody else, allowed to walk a few steps, it will not be a sin worthy of penance.

ten

MOHESH[*]

I

The name of the village is Kaashipur. The village is small,
the local zamindar even smaller, yet under his thumb his
subjects cannot let out a squeak, such is his power.

It was his younger son's birthday ceremony. Tarkaratna
was returning home at 2 in the afternoon, after completing
the ceremonial rituals. Though *baishakh* was nearing its end,
the sky was clear of even the vestige of a cloud; it seemed
as though fire was raining down from the drought-laden sky.

Ahead, the village commons stretched endlessly towards the
horizon, burnt, baked and cracked into a million crevices, and
from those million crevices, from the earth's heart, her very
life blood vaporized ceaselessly. Just staring at that serpentine
and constant upward motion of the heat-waves, like dancing
tongues of fire, the head reeled, one felt intoxicated.

[*]Translated from the original with the same title 'Mohesh', in *SSS*, Vol.
2, pp. 1726–31.

At the very end of the commons, just next to the path, was Gofur Julaha's[1] hut. The earthen outer wall had collapsed and its courtyard had merged with the path while its *antahpur*[2] had quietly submitted its honour and modesty to the compassionate gaze of the passers-by, and relieved itself of care.

Standing under the shade of a *pitoli* tree, Tarkaratna raised his voice and hollered, 'Orey o Goffraa, I say, are you home?'

His ten-year-old daughter came and stood at the door and said, 'Baba? What for? He has a fever.'

'Fever! Call that bastard! Stony-hearted! Mlecchha!'

Roused by all the raucous commotion, Gofur Miyan emerged from the hut shivering with fever, and came to the caller. Growing just next to the broken-down outer wall was an old *baablaa* tree. Tethered to one of its branches was a bull. Pointing to this presence, Tarkaratna said, 'What's all this, let's hear? This is a Hindu village, the zamindar is a Brahmin, don't you remember?' Gofur understood that since a face was flushed scarlet from the sun and with wrath, only heated words could come from it. But as the cause escaped Gofur's comprehension, he merely stared blankly.

Tarkaratna said, 'When I passed here this morning I saw him tied at this spot, and now when I am returning, I still see him tied here. If there is any cattle-slaughter, the *karta*[3] will bury you alive. He is not an ordinary Brahmin.'

'What can I do, Babathakur, I am in a real fix. I have got fever since the last few days now. I would take him on his rope and give him two bites to eat, but my head reels

---

[1] A Muslim weaver
[2] Inner quarters
[3] Master of the household

and I keep falling.'

'Then untie him, he will go and feed on his own.'

'Where will I leave him, Babathakur! People haven't finished harvesting the paddy, the sheaves are still lying in the fields. The straw hasn't been stored, the furrows in the commons have all burnt up, there is not even a handful of grass; he will go and eat someone's paddy, he will go and scatter someone's straw stack. How can I just turn him loose, Babathakur?'

Tarkaratna softened a little, and said, 'If you can't turn him loose, at least tie him up in the shade and give him two bundles of straw—he can munch for a while. Your daughter hasn't cooked rice? Give him some starch and water—he can have a manger of that.'

Gofur did not answer. He stared helplessly at Tarkaratna and only a deep sigh emerged from his mouth.

Tarkaratna said, 'Even that you don't have? What did you do with the straw? Whatever you got in your share you sold and worshipped your own stomach? You could not keep a bundle or two for your bullock? Bloody butcher!'

This cruel accusation seemed to stop Gofur's very speech. After a little while, he said very slowly, 'I had got a measure—a *kahan*[4] worth of straw—but kartamohashoyey confiscated it, saying that it was to pay for last year's deficit. I cried and cried, fell at his feet and said, babumoshai, you are the judge, where will I go from your kingdom—just give me maybe ten *pon*[5] of straw. The thatch has no fresh straw, there is just one room, where the two of us—father and daughter—stay,

---

[4] A unit of measurement; it specifically stands for fourteen bundles of straw.
[5] One pon equals eighty pieces (*aanti*); sixteen pon equals one kahan.

we will make do with some palm leaves stuck into the roof and manage somehow during the coming monsoons, but my Mohesh will simply die for want of food.'

Tarkaratna laughed and mocked, '*Issh!*[6] To have lovingly named him Mohesh! I will die of laughter!'

But this taunt did not fall on Gofur's ears, he went on saying, 'But the judge did not feel any pity. He gave us enough paddy to last us two months, but all the straw went straight to the big *sarkar*. My Mohesh did not get even one straw.' Gofur's voice grew heavy with the weight of tears during this recital, but Tarkaratna did not feel any compassion. He said, 'You're a fine one! You will eat it all, but you don't want to give anything to the landlord. Will the zamindar feed you from his personal resources? You live in *Ram Rajatya*[7], but you are all *chhotolok*, so you all badmouth him with your dying breath.'

Gofur said shamefacedly, 'Why should we badmouth him? We do not badmouth him. But from where shall we give, you tell us. I work in about four bighas of land as a shareholder, but with two years of drought one after the other—the paddy just shrivelled up standing in the paddy fields. Father and daughter—together we don't get enough to eat even twice a day. Look at the hut. When it rains, I sit in the corner of the room with the girl, we don't even have enough room to stretch out our legs. Just look at Mohesh, you can count his ribs—do give two kahans of straw as a loan Thakurmoshai, I can then give him some good filling meals for a few days.' As he said this, Gofur plonked down right at the feet of the

---

[6] An expression of pity, here, pretentious in nature.

[7] The mythical kingdom ruled by perfect dharma, brought about by Lord Rama.

Brahmin. Tarkaratna stepped back two paces in a flash, and said, 'Just die! Are you going to touch me?'

'No, no, Babathakur, why should I touch you—I won't touch you. But give me two kahans of straw this time. You have all of four big stacks of straw, I saw them the other day—if you give just this much you won't even realize it's gone. There's no harm if we starve to death, but my Mohesh is a gentle creature, he cannot speak, he only stares and tears fall from his eyes.'

Tarkaratna said, 'You'll take a loan; how will you repay it?'

Suddenly hopeful, Gofur said eagerly, 'I will repay it somehow, Babathakur, I wouldn't cheat you.'

Tarkaratna imitated Gofur's anxious yet eager tones, 'I wouldn't cheat you! I will pay back somehow! Amorous lover! Get lost, move, get out of my way. It's getting late, I have to go home.' So saying, he took a step forward, preparing to leave, but suddenly stepped fearfully backwards and said angrily, 'Drop down dead! He is coming at me shaking his horns, is he going to stick them into me or what?'

Gofur got to his feet. He pointed to the little bundle of wet rice and fruits the thakur was carrying in his hand, and said, 'He's got the scent, he wants to eat a handful.'

'He wants to eat? Just so. The peasant's bullock is just like the peasant. Can't get straw, wants to eat rice and bananas! Tie him up away from the path! Such horns, I can see someone will get murdered one of these days.' So saying, Tarkaratna skirted round danger and hurried away.

Gofur turned his gaze away from him and brought it back to Mohesh's face, and stared at it for a while in silence—at the deep dark eyes that were so full of pain and hunger. He said, 'He did not give you just a fistful? They have a lot, still they do not give. Let them not give…,' his throat closed convulsively, and then from his eyes fell teardrops. He came close and stroking Mohesh's neck, head and back tenderly, he began whispering, 'Mohesh, you are my son, you have served us for eight years and now you have grown old. I cannot give you a full meal, large enough to fill your stomach, but you know how much I love you.'

In response, Mohesh stretched out his neck and closed his eyes in contentment. Gofur rubbed his teardrops off from the bull's back and continued to whisper, 'The zamindar has robbed you of your food, the little strip of pasture next to the cemetery he has leased out because of his greed for money. In such a hard year, tell me how I can keep you alive. If I let you loose, you'll bring down someone's straw stack, you'll eat up someone's plantain tree, what am I am going to do with you? You have no physical strength left, in this country nobody wants you, they tell me to sell you off at the cattle-mart…' Just saying these words in his own heart made the tears fall again. Gofur wiped them off with his hand, looked this way and that furtively, sneaked behind the broken hut, brought out some discoloured, old straw, and placed it before Mohesh's muzzle. He said in a low voice, 'Here, quickly eat this baba, if you are late, again there will…'

'Baba!'

'Why maa?'

'Come and eat rice…,' with these words Ameena stood at the threshold, just looked on for a moment, and then said, 'You've once again pulled out straw from the thatch to give Mohesh, Baba?'

Gofur was afraid of just this happening, and he murmured shamefacedly, 'It was old and rotten straw maa, it was falling off all by itself.'

'But from inside the room I did hear you pulling it out from the thatch?'

'No, no, not exactly pulling it out.'

'But the wall will collapse Baba...'

Gofur remained silent. Who knew better than himself that this room was the only thing they had left, the rest had all collapsed, and if he continued like this, even this would not last through the coming rains? Yet, maybe a few more days could be tackled in this way?

The daughter said, 'Baba, I have served the rice, wash your hands and come and eat.'

Gofur said, 'Maa, just give me the rice-starch, let me just feed him this little bit.'

'There is no starch today, Baba, it has dried up in the vessel.'

'None?' Gofur fell silent. In these days of dire poverty, even a ten-year-old girl had understood that nothing could be wasted. He washed his hands and came and stood inside the room. On a brass plate, his daughter had set out his rice and vegetables, and had taken rice for herself in a shallow earthenware bowl. Gofur looked and looked and then said very softly, 'Ameena, my body has started feeling cold again, maa—is it good to eat on top of a fever?'

His daughter said anxiously, 'But a while back you said you were feeling hungry?'

'Then? Maybe then there was no fever.'

'Then shall I put it away, you can eat it in the evening?'

'But if I eat cold food, my condition will worsen.'

Ameena said, 'Then, what shall I do?'

Gofur became immersed in deep thought, and then suddenly with the air of solving a really difficult problem, he said, 'Why don't you do something maa? Give whatever there is on the plate to Mohesh. In the evening, won't you be able to boil me a handful of rice, Ameena?' In reply, Ameena raised her eyes to her father's face and looked at him for a little while, then lowered her face, slowly nodded her head and said, 'I can, Baba.'

Gofur went red in the face. From afar, perhaps one more Presence noted this little charade enacted between the father and the daughter.

II

Some five to six days later, an ailing Gofur was sitting on his verandah with a worried face. His Mohesh had not come back home since the previous day. As he was completely incapacitated, Ameena had been hunting for him everywhere all morning. When the day was waning, she came and reported, 'Do you know Baba, the Manik Ghosh family have sent our Mohesh to the thana.'

Gofur was disbelieving, 'Huh, crazy girl!'

'But Baba, it is true. Their servant told me, "tell your father to go and search for him in the Dariapur cattle pen".'

'What had he done?'

'He had entered their garden and damaged their greenery.'

Gofur sat in stunned silence. He had been imagining all sorts of disasters that might have befallen Mohesh, but he had not feared this. He was as harmless as he was poor, and he had never expected that his neighbours might heap such harsh punishment upon him, particularly Manik Ghosh. He was famous for his deep devotion for the Brahmin and the bovine.

His daughter said, 'Baba, it is almost evening, won't you

go and fetch Mohesh?'

Gofur said, 'No.'

'But they told me that after three days they will sell him off at the cattle-mart?'

Gofur said, 'Let them.'

Ameena had no precise idea of what exactly was this cattle-mart, but she had often noticed that whenever it was mentioned with reference to Mohesh, her father used to become extremely agitated. However, today she did not utter anything further but went away slowly.

Under the dark cover of the night, Gofur arrived at Bangshi's shop and laid his brass plate under Bangshi's perch saying, 'Khudo, you have to give me a rupee—.' Bangshi was very familiar with the weight and other particulars of this object. In the last two years, he had lent a rupee at least five times against it as security. Therefore, this time too, he did not ask any questions or raise any objection to the request.

The next day, Mohesh was once again to be seen at the usual location. The same shade of the *baablaa* tree, the same rope, the same post, the same grassless environ, the same wet and eager appeal in the deep, black, hungry eyes. An elderly Muslim was surveying him with extremely sharp eyes. Some distance away, Gofur Miyan was sitting silently with his knees drawn up to his chest. After the examination, the old man took out a ten-rupee note, opened its folds, smoothened it out repeatedly, and held it out saying, 'I won't haggle over small change; here, take the whole note.'

Gofur put out his hand, took the note, and remained as silently seated as before. However, the moment the two men who had accompanied the old man moved to loosen the rope tethering the bull, he shot straight to his feet and uttered aggressively, 'Don't touch the rope, I am warning you, don't dare touch it I say, you will regret it.'

They were startled. The old man, astonished, asked, 'Why?'

Gofur replied in the same angry tone, 'What's the why for? I won't sell my property—it's my wish.' And he flung away the note.

They still persisted, 'But yesterday, you took an advance while you were returning home…?'

'Here, take your advance back!' and Gofur, taking the two rupees out of his waistband, tossed them noisily on the ground. The old man, sensing a quarrel brewing, smiled and said quietly, 'You want to pump me harder to squeeze out a little more, is that so? *Oye*, there, put two more rupees in his daughter's hand to buy snacks to eat. That's right, isn't it?'

'No.'

'But do you know that no one will give even half a paise more?'

'No.'

The old man said testily, 'What no? Only the skin will sell for some price, what else is there of any value?'

'Tauba! Tauba!' A harshly abusive expletive exploded from Gofur's mouth. He ran into his room, and began to yell out threats of sending for the zamindar's men to beat them with shoes if they did not leave the village that very instant.

Faced with a row, the men left, but shortly after, Gofur received summons from the zamindar's office. Gofur realized that the news had reached the karta's ears.

There were both respectable and disrespectful individuals sitting around the zamindar's office. Shibu-babu, with reddened eyes, said, 'Gofra, I am at a loss to decide what kind of punishment to give you. Are you aware of exactly where you live?'

Gofur folded his hands and said, 'I know. I do not have enough to eat, otherwise I would not have said no to whatever fine you chose to impose on me.'

Everyone was surprised. They all knew this man to be both stubborn and bad-tempered. He said tearfully, 'I will never do such a thing again, karta.' So saying, he twisted both his ears with his hands, rubbed his nose along the entire length of the floor of the court, and then stood up.

Shibu-babu, in a kind voice, said, 'Okay, that will do. Don't ever do such a thing again.'

Having heard the whole narrative everyone present expressed deep shock. They were all unanimous and convinced about the fact that an enormous sin had only been averted because of the zamindar's holy influence. Tarkaratna was present too. He pontificated on the shastric explanation of the consequences of cow slaughter. The assembly was further illuminated as to why the residence of irreligious mlecchha communities was prohibited even on the fringes of a village, and the local horizon of knowledge expanded materially.

Gofur made no retort to the taunts and revilements flung at him. In all sincerity, he accepted the humiliation and all the rebukes as veritably deserved and returned home satisfied. He obtained some rice-starch from his neighbours and fed Mohesh. He murmured many soft blandishments to him and stroked his head, his horns, his body.

III

The month of jyastha came to an end. At the end of baishakh, the sun had just begun to reveal his face of pitiless destruction. Unless one actually gazed at the present sky, one would be entirely incapable of realizing the fearful, stern cruelty that now stood revealed. The sky was completely devoid of even a drop of pity. Even to think that this appearance could change by as much as a hair, that this sky could be weighed down by dark rain-bearing clouds that could soothe and nurture, seemed a fearful impossibility. The constant rain of fire falling from the burning white-hot sky seemed inexhaustible, endless. Until everything was burnt to a cinder, it would not stop.

On one such day, at two o'clock in the afternoon, Gofur came back home. He was not used to the life of a daily-wage labourer who worked for other people. Moreover, it had been a mere four to five days that he had shaken off his fever. His body was still as weak as it was worn out. Still, he had started searching for work since morning. But though the fierce midday sun had certainly hammered at him, nothing had materialized from his efforts. Consumed with thirst, hunger and weariness, he was almost seeing black; he called out from the yard, 'Ameena, is the rice ready?'

His daughter emerged with slow steps from inside the room and wordlessly held on to the post.

Receiving no answer, Gofur shouted, 'Is the rice done? What did you say—not done? Let's hear why!'

'There are no rice grains, Baba!'

'No rice grains! Why didn't you tell me in the morning?'

'But I did tell you last night.'

Gofur pulled a face and mimicked, 'But I told you last night! Can anyone remember if something is said at night?' His rage doubled, fed on his own harsh tone. He twisted his face even further and said, 'No wonder there are no rice grains. What if the sick old father has not eaten, the great big hussy will shovel rice down her throat four to five times a day! From now on I will lock up the grains before I leave.

Give, give a bowl of water—my chest is simply bursting with thirst! Now say there is no water either.'

Ameena stood rooted to the spot with her head bent. After waiting for a few moments, when Gofur finally realized that there was not even water in the house to slake his thirst, he could not control himself any more. He swiftly went to her, dealt her a resounding slap across her cheek, and said, 'Useless, wicked girl, what do you do the whole day? So many people die, and you don't!'

The girl did not utter a word, she lifted the empty pot and wiping her eyes, went out into the burning afternoon. The moment she was out of sight, Gofur's heart was impaled upon a steel shaft. Only he knew how he had brought up this motherless girl. He remembered that this affectionate, hard-working and patient girl was not at fault. Even while the little rice from the field lasted, they still did not manage to eat two square meals a day. Sometimes it was a single meal, sometimes they did not get even that. It was as impossible as it was false to accuse her of eating rice five or six times a day. Even the reason why there was no water for drinking was not unknown to him. The two or three tanks in the village were totally dry. Shivcharan-babu's tank in his backyard was not open to everybody, and there was very little water in the other waterbodies in the village, accessed through deep little holes around which there were always large crowds fighting for space. Especially as she was a Muslim, this little girl was not even allowed near the water. After much pleading and begging from afar, somebody would take a little pity and pour a little water into her pot, and only this she brought home. He knew all this. Maybe today there was no water, or perhaps in the melee, nobody had the time to be kind to his daughter. His own eyes filled with tears, knowing something of this nature must have happened today. At this point the zamindar's *pyadas*[8], like messengers of Yama, came right into his yard and yelled, 'Gofraa! Are you home?'

Gofur answered in a bitter tone, 'Yes. Why?'

'Babumoshai has summoned you, come.'

Gofur said, 'I haven't had any food, I'll come later.'

The pyada could not tolerate such insolence. He let fly an ugly expletive and said, 'The babu's orders are to drag you along while peppering you with shoe-strokes.'

For the second time, Gofur lost his self-command; he too uttered an abuse and declared, 'In the Empress's domain, nobody is anybody's slave. I pay taxes for staying here, I will not go.'

However, in this world, for someone so small to give vent to such an enormous excuse was not just futile, but dangerous as well. The only saving grace was that such a feeble voice could not reach such powerful ears—otherwise both his night's sleep as well as his daily food would have escaped him. It is not necessary to narrate in detail what happened after this, but when Gofur returned from the zamindar's headquarters to his hut after an hour, and silently lay down, his eyes and mouth had swollen up. The reason for this harsh punishment was chiefly Mohesh. After Gofur had left his house, he too had snapped his rope and had invaded the zamindar's flower garden and not only eaten the flowering shrubs, but had also scattered and wasted the husked rice that was drying in the sun. Finally, when there had been attempts to catch him, he had knocked down the Babu's young daughter and had

---

[8]A policeman belonging to lower orders of the official hierarchy.

made good his escape. Such an event was not new, and had happened previously too, but he had been let off as he was so poor. Had he, like before, grovelled before the zamindar as he had always done in the past, he might have been forgiven. But the zamindar had not been able to stomach the incredible insolence of a subject who had openly declared that he paid taxes and was nobody's slave. He had not made the smallest sound or protested under the severe beating and insults, and he was totally silent even after his return. That he was hungry and thirsty had also faded from his memory. But his heart was burning like the high-noon furnace raging across the skies outside. He lost count of the time as it passed, and only sprang to his feet when he suddenly heard his daughter's startled scream in the courtyard. He raced outside and saw that Ameena lay sprawling on the ground, and the water was pouring from the broken pot. Mohesh had put his head down and was sucking up the water like a thirsty desert. Before the flicker of an eyelid, Gofur lost all his senses. He had removed the head of the plough for repair the day before. He grabbed it now with both hands and struck Mohesh's bent head with great force.

Mohesh attempted to lift his head just once, and then his enfeebled and skeletal frame collapsed on the ground. A few teardrops fell from the corners of his eyes, a few drops of blood trickled from his ears. His entire body shuddered once or twice, and then stretching out his front and back legs as far as they would go, Mohesh breathed his last.

Ameena burst into tears and said, 'What have you done, Baba, our Mohesh has died!'

Gofur did not move, did not respond, still as stone, he just gazed unblinkingly into another pair of open, deep, dark eyes.

Within an hour or two, the news spread and the leather-workers gathered, slung the tied Mohesh onto bamboo poles, and left for the slaughter-ground. Gofur shivered and shut his eyes when he saw the long gleaming knives in their hands, but he did not say a word.

The neighbours told Gofur that the zamindar had sent word to Tarkaratna for advice as to procedure, and maybe he would have to sell his hut to provide the money for penance.

Gofur did not vouchsafe any answer to these statements too, he just kept sitting with his head on his drawn-up knees.

Very late into the night, Gofur roused his daughter from sleep and said, 'Ameena, come, let's go—' She had gone to sleep on the plinth of the hut; she sat up rubbing her eyes, and said, 'Where, Baba?'

Gofur said, 'To work in the jute mills at Phoolbedey.'

The girl stared in amazement. Before this, even when in dire poverty, her father had refused to work in the jute mills. She had heard him say many times that there, religion and honour of women were endangered.

Gofur said, 'Maa, don't delay, come, we have to walk a very long way.'

As Ameena was taking the small vessel for drinking water and her father's brass plate, Gofur forbade her, 'Let those things be, they will be needed for my Mohesh's penance.'

In the profound darkness of the night, he left holding his daughter's hand. He had no relatives in this village, there was nothing to say to anybody. He crossed the yard and then suddenly halted under the baablaa tree at the roadside and wept aloud. Raising his face towards the star-studded black sky, he said, 'Allah, punish me as much as you want, but my Mohesh died thirsty. Nobody kept even a bit of grazing land for him. They did not allow him to eat the grass you have provided, to drink the water you have bestowed; never, ever forgive them.'

eleven

ABHAAGI'S HEAVEN[*]

*T*he elderly wife of Thakurdas Mukhujje passed away after suffering from a week-long fever. Her spouse, the venerable Mukhopadhyay, was very well-off, chiefly due to his grain (rice) business. The mood was almost festive at the funeral— his four sons, four daughters, their children, the sons-in-law, the neighbours and the servants—were all present. The entire village turned out to see the funeral procession carrying the dead body to the cremation grounds. The weeping daughters had applied sindoor thickly to her head and red *alta*[1] to her feet. The daughters-in-law had applied sandalwood paste to her forehead, decked their mother-in-law in the costliest of saris, and with the ends of their saris, gathered in the last bit of the dust from her feet. The flowers, leaves, incense, garlands and the general hubbub did not convey the mood of grief— it felt more like a fresh journey undertaken by the mistress

---

[*]Translated from the original 'Abhaagir Swarga', in *SSS*, Vol. 2, pp. 1733–38.
[1]Red dye applied on the reams of the feet of married women; it is a symbol of their being married.

of the household to her husband's house after fifty years. The old Mukhopadhyay, with a calm face bade his lifelong companion adieu, wiped a few tears discreetly, and consoled the grieving daughters and daughters-in-law. The bright morning sky reverberated with the roars of '*Hari bol*' from the entire village as they all moved on in procession. Another creature followed them at a little distance. She was Kaangaali's mother. She was on her way to the village market with a few eggplants plucked from near her hut. She was transfixed at the sight that met her eyes. She forgot about going to the market, she forgot about the few eggplants tied into her sari-end, and constantly wiping her tears, followed behind the procession right up to the cremation ground. The cremation ground was located at one end of the village, on the banks of the river Garuda. From the morning, all the necessary paraphernalia—piles of wood, pieces of sandalwood, clarified butter, honey, incense—had been accumulating there. Kaangaali's mother was a low-caste, a Duley,[2] and she did not dare to go too close. She stood on a small hillock, a little distance away and watched the last rites from the beginning to the end with interested and fascinated eyes. When the dead body was placed on a wide and long pyre, her eyes were deeply soothed by the lady's beautifully alta-reddened feet: she wished she could run up to the pyre, collect a drop of the alta and gently touch it to her forehead. When, accompanied by many full-throated 'Hari bols', the son's hand set the sacred, consecrated fire to the pyre, tears poured down her face. She kept repeating inwardly, 'Oh mother, you are going to heaven, you are so fortunate. Please bless me too, that even I can get the consecrated fire from Kaangaali's

---

[2]Untouchable, low-caste cultivators

hand.' The consecrated fire from a son's hand! Hardly a trivial thing! To leave the world surrounded by her husband, sons, daughters, grandsons, granddaughters, servants, relatives—to go to heaven when her household was at its apogee—Kaangaali's mother's breast swelled with emotion—the enormity of such good fortune was beyond her comprehension. Heavy smoke, casting a blue shadow on the ground, was rising into the air from the recently-lit pyre: Kaangaali's mother could see a small chariot within the smoke quite clearly. All over it were scores of pictures, and there were beautiful leaves and creepers trailing from the chariot's crown. Somebody was sitting inside, and though the face was invisible, the mark of the sindoor could be seen clearly, and also her beautiful alta-reddened feet. Kaangaali's mother's upturned eyes were streaming with tears, when a fourteen to fifteen-year-old boy came and tugged at her sari-end, 'You're standing here, won't ye cook rice?'

The mother started and looked around, 'In a little bit!' She suddenly pointed with her finger, 'Baba, look look, *bamun*[3]-maa is going to heaven mounted on that chariot!'

The boy with a surprised expression on his face, looked up and asked, 'Where?' He stared a little, then said, 'Are you mad? That is just smoke.' Annoyed, he then said, 'It is afternoon. Don't I feel hungry?' But all at once he noticed his mother's tears and exclaimed, 'You're crying because that Brahmin mistress is dead?'

Kaangaali's mother came back to herself. She felt a little embarrassed at her overflowing emotions for the death of someone she barely knew. She even felt a little anxious about its possible malevolent effect on her son. She quickly wiped

---

[3] *Bamun* or Brahmin

her eyes, tried to smile and said, 'Why should I cry? The smoke has entered my eyes.'

'Huh! Smoke never got into your eyes! Ye were crying!'

The mother did not protest anymore. She got down into the river holding her son's hand, took a bath, bathed her son too—and then both returned home. She did not manage to see the remaining funereal rituals.

II

Vidhaatapurush[4] is not just amused at most parents' stupidity at the naming of their children—he objects strongly. And so their names mock them all through their lives. Kaangaali's mother's life history is quite short, but her short lifespan has been spared the mockery of the Almighty. Her mother had died after giving birth to this daughter, so her father angrily named her 'Abhaagi'—the unfortunate one. She had no mother, her father was always away, catching fish in the river, oblivious to day or night. It was a miracle that the tiny Abhaagi remained alive and grew up to be Kaangaaali's mother. She was married to a man called Rasik Baagh—Baagh, as in tiger. He came across his tigress, and very soon moved with her to another village. Abhaagi remained with her misfortune and her infant son in her own village.

That little Kaangaali has now grown to be fifteen. He has just begun to learn basket-weaving; and Abhaagi's hope is that if she can battle with her misfortune for a year more, her hardships will cease to be. No one else can comprehend this bottomless sorrow, apart from the One who had inflicted it.

Kaangaali came back from the water tank following his

---

[4]Fate, destiny, divinity

after-meal ablutions, and saw his mother storing the remaining food in an earthenware vessel. Surprised, he inquired, 'Won't ye eat, Maa?'

She said, 'Now it is very late, I'm not hungry.'

The son did not believe her, 'Yes, indeed ye aren't hungry! Let me see the vessel?'

His mother has used this excuse many times before, and Kaangaali only believed her when he had checked the vessel for himself. There was enough rice for one person. So he sat happily on her lap. Boys his age did not generally do this. However, because he had constantly ailed as a child, he had never had much of an opportunity to leave his mother's lap and mingle with boys his own age. He has had to remain there and make up for all his desire for play. Kaangaali put his arm around her neck, and his face against hers, then started and said, 'Maa, you're warm—why did ye stand under the sun to watch the burning of the corpse? Why did ye then again go for a bath? The burning of the corpse, ye—' The mother quickly placed her palm over the son's mouth, 'Shame, never say "corpse". It's a sin. The virtuous sati has mounted the chariot and has gone to heaven.'

The son was suspicious, 'Maa, you keep saying that! No one goes to heaven in a chariot.'

The mother said, 'I saw with my own eyes Kaangaali, bamun-maa was sitting in the chariot. Everyone saw her red feet.'

'Everyone saw?'

'*Everyone* saw.'

Kaangaali leaned on his mother's chest and thought about it. He was naturally prone to believing her—since childhood he had been trained to believe whatever she said. So when his mother said that everyone had seen such a big event, he felt

Saratchandra Chattopadhyay

that there was nothing unbelievable about it. He said slowly after a little while, 'Ye will also go to heaven, then? That day, Bindi's mother was telling Rakhal's (paternal) aunt that there is no one as pure as Kaanglaa's mother in Duley-*paadaa*.'

Kaangaali's mother was silent, and Kaangaali continued to say slowly, 'When father left ye, so many people advised ye to marry again, but ye said "no". Ye said, "if Kaangaali lives, then my misfortune will pass, why should I marry again?" But Maa, if ye had entered into another nikash, where would I have lived? I would perhaps have died of starvation.'

The mother hugged her son close to her chest with both her hands. Indeed, there had been many who had told her to do just that, and when she had flatly refused, she had suffered a lot of personal attacks. As these memories returned, tears fell from Abhaagi's eyes. The son wiped them away with his hand, and said, 'Let me spread out the *kantha*[5], Maa, lie down.'

Maa was silent. Kaangaali spread out the kantha, took down a small pillow from the hammock, and pulled his mother over to the bed for some rest. His mother said, 'Kaangaali, skip going to work today.'

The proposal that he bunk work really appealed to Kaangaali, but he said, 'But they won't give the two pice for snacks.'

'Let them not give—come let me tell ye a *roopkatha*[6].'

Kaangaali did not need further temptation; he immediately lay down close to his mother and said, 'Tell me. The king's son, the *kotal*'s son and the *pakshiraj*[7] horse—' Abhaagi began her

---

[5] A traditional hand-stitched blanket using layers of cotton cloth.
[6] Fairy tale
[7] 'Kotal' is the colloquial Bengali word for 'kotwal', the chief military officer. The *pakshiraj* is the winged horse in Bengali fables.

story with 'The king's son, the kotal's son and the pakshiraj horse—'

These were the tales she had heard from other people, and she had herself retold them a countless number of times. But after a little while, 'the king's son, the kotal's son' vanished from the tale—she started to invent her own tales not learnt from anyone else. The more her fever increased, and the hot blood rushed to her head with increasing rapidity, the more she kept spinning out newer and newer tales. There was no end, no pause, to their flow. As he heard these, the slight body of Kaangaali would now and again quiver with intense emotion. He would hug his mother and burrow into her body in fear, amazement and joy.

Outside, the day closed, the sun set and the darkness of the evening advanced over the world; but inside the hut there was no lamp lit today, no one got up to perform the householder's last duties. Only the sick mother's uninterrupted murmurs filled the silent son's ears with sweetness and magic. It was the tale of the cremation ground and the procession going there. That chariot, those two red feet, the ascent to heaven. How the sad husband had given the last dust from his feet before sending her off, how the sons had borne the body with cries of 'Hari bol', and then the fire from the hands of the sons. 'That was not fire, Kaangaali, that was *Hari* himself! That smoke filling the sky was not smoke but the heavenly chariot! Kaangaalicharan! My son!'

'Yes, Maa?'

'If I get the fire from your hands, even I will go to heaven.'

Kaangaali could barely manage an indistinct, 'Nah! Don't say such things!'

The mother possibly did not even hear this. She let out a

feverish breath and said, 'Then nobody will be able to loathe me because I am a low-caste, nobody will be able to stop me because I am poor. Issh! The fire from the son's hands—the chariot will have to come.'

The son, with his face on hers, said brokenly, 'Don't say such things, Maa, don't say them—I get very frightened.'

The mother said, 'And look Kaangaali, get your father here just once, he must give me the last dust of his feet before sending me off, just like that. Just like that there must be alta on my feet and sindoor on my head—but who will put them on? Ye will put it on, won't ye Kaangaali? Ye are my son, ye are my daughter, ye are everything to me!' And she hugged her son close to her.

III

The last chapters of Abhaagi's life were rapidly drawing to a close. It was quite short. I think—not even thirty years—and it ended like it had begun, negligently. The kaviraj[8] lived in another village. Kaangaali went there and wept, fell at his feet, and finally pawned a pot for a rupee and gave it to him as fee. The kaviraj did not come himself but gave him perhaps four pills. So much went into them—tree-bark, honey, dry ginger, the juice of basil. But Abhaagi was annoyed and complained, 'Why did ye pawn a pot without asking me?' She accepted the pills in her cupped hands but flung them into the small kiln. She said, 'If I am to get well, I will get well with this. In houses of the Bagdi-Duley castes, nobody survives by taking medicines.'

---

[8]One well-versed in herbology and other fields of study involving traditional medicine.

Two to three days went by like this. The neighbours heard the news and came to see her. They gave recipes for treatment—water that had been used to wash a deer's horns, a joined *kadi*[9] which had to be burnt, then crushed, mixed with honey, and then to be licked by the patient—and similar such suggestions. Then they would leave for their work. The young Kaangaali became so very visibly perturbed that his mother pulled him to her and consoled him, 'Kaviraj's pills did not do any good, how will their suggestions help? I will get better on my own.'

Kaangaali wept and said, 'Ye didn't take those pills, Maa, ye threw them away in the kiln. Does anyone get better on one's own?'

Abhaagi said, 'I'll get better on my own. Now let me see—ye boil some rice and vegetables.'

Kaangaali, for the first time in his life, began to cook rice with inexpert hands. He could not drain the starch or dole out the rice properly. His kiln would not light—water kept dripping into it and only smoke billowed out. When he tried to ladle out the rice, it scattered all over the plate. The mother's eyes filled with tears. She tried to get up once, but she could not sit up, and flopped back onto the bed. After he had finished eating, she drew him close and began to tell him how to cook properly, but her faint voice stopped midway, and tears poured down her eyes.

Ishwar, the village barber knew how to check the pulse: that morning he examined Abhaagi's pulse and before her eyes, his face grew very serious. He heaved a sigh and finally shook his head before leaving. Kaangaali's mother understood

---

[9]Cowry shells

the meaning of all this, but she did not feel frightened. She called her son to her when all had left, and said, 'Now will ye call him once, baba?'

'Who, Maa?'

'Him, the one who has gone to the other village—'

Kaangaali understood and said, 'Do ye mean Baba?'

Abhaagi was silent.

Kaangaali said, 'Why will he come, Maa?'

Abhaagi herself felt doubtful, but nevertheless she said hesitantly, 'Go and tell him, Maa just wants a little dust from his feet.'

Being keen that Kaangaali goes that very instant, she caught hold of his hand and said, 'Cry a little baba, tell him Maa is leaving.'

After a little pause, she said, 'On your way back, get some alta from the barber's wife, Kaangaali. She is very fond of me; if ye take my name she'll give it to ye for free.'

There were many who were fond of her. Kaangaali had heard of these objects in so many contexts ever since his mother had fallen ill with fever, that now he dissolved into tears as he set out on his journey.

IV

By the time Rasik Duley arrived the next day, Abhaagi was almost unconscious. The shadow of death was clearly on her face, her gaze was fixed on an unknown country, far removed from the cares of this world. Kaangaali wept and said, 'Oh Maa! Baba has come—don't ye want the dust from his feet!'

His mother may or may not have understood this. But her deep desire must have stirred her into consciousness, like compulsive actions guided by long traditions. This traveller ready for the last journey, stretched out a lifeless arm outside the bed, palm upwards.

Rasik stood like one bewildered. That in this world the dust of his feet had any value, that somebody could want it, was beyond his imagination. Bindi's paternal aunt was standing close by, she said, 'Give, do give, baba—some dust from your feet.'

Rasik came forward. In his entire life, he had not given his wife love, food or clothes, had never even enquired after her, but now, on her deathbed, as he was about to give her the dust from his feet, he began to cry.

Rakhal's mother said, 'Why did such a *sati-lakshmi* take birth in a Duley household instead of being born in some Brahmin or Kayeth's family! Now make some provisions for her. She was so greedy for a little fire from Kaanglaa's hands that she threw her life away.'

I do not know what the God of Abhaagi's misfortune may have thought of this statement, but young Kaangaali felt these words pierce his heart like an arrow.

The entire day passed, as did the first hours of the night, but Kaangaali's mother did not wait for the dawn. Who knew, perhaps there was no heavenly chariot for someone from such a low caste, maybe such persons had to walk in the dark on this last journey. But it was clear that before the night had ended, she had left this world.

There was a *sriphal* tree growing near the fence. Rasik borrowed an axe and had barely touched the tree with it, when the zamindar's guard came running up from somewhere and resoundingly slapped his face. He pulled away the axe, and said, '*Sala*[10], is this your father's tree that you are chopping it down?'

---

[10] *Sala* is an abusive term that is equal to 'scoundrel' or 'rascal'.

Rasik nursed his cheek, while Kaangaali said tearfully, 'Oh, but this is a tree my mother planted with her own hands, *darowanji*.[11] Why did ye hit Baba for nothing?'

The Hindustani guard spat another unmentionable abuse at him too, and would have hit him, but desisted as he was scared that Kaangaali, having had touched his mother's corpse and therefore unclean, would also pollute him. A crowd gathered at the sound of loud voices, and nobody denied that Rasik should have taken permission before attempting to cut the tree down. But they too began to plead with the guard to kindly give an order. Whoever had come to visit Abhaagi, had known about her last wish, for she had individually held everyone's hands and had stated her desire.

The guard was not to be won over: he shook his head and hands and declared that such strategies would not work on him.

The zamindar was not a local. But he had a *kacheri*[12] in this village, headed by the *gomostah*, Adhar Roy. When the others were pleading with the Hindustani guard fruitlessly, Kaangaali ran with all his might to the kacheri. He was convinced that if he could tell the highest authority of the harsh and unjust treatment they had just suffered, justice would be done, and anyway, he had heard from other people that guards desired bribes. Alas, for such inexperience! He had no idea of the real nature of the zamindars of Bengal and their office-bearers. The young boy, in his bewilderment and grief at losing his mother, had run right up to the house. Adhar Roy had just emerged from the house: he had completed his Brahminic rituals and

---

[11]Security officer
[12]Office; and the officer is normally called *gomostah*.

had taken a little refreshment a brief while back, but he was both surprised and angry at the sudden intrusion— 'Who is it?'

'I'm Kaangaali. Darowanji has hit my Baba.'

'He is right. The bastard hasn't paid tax or what?'

Kaangaali said, 'No babumoshai, my Baba was cutting a tree—my Maa is dead—,' he could go no further and burst into tears. Adhar grew very irritated with all this weeping the first thing in the morning. The boy had touched a corpse, God only knew if he had touched anything here. He scolded, 'If your Maa is dead, then go, and stand below. Hey, who is here, just sprinkle some holy water[13] here! What caste are you?'

Kaangaali fearfully backed down into the courtyard, and said, 'We are Duley.'

Adhar said, 'Duley! Why should the corpse of a Duley need wood?'

Kaangaali said, 'Maa had asked me to set fire to her pyre! You ask anyone babumoshai, Maa has told everybody, everyone has heard it!' As he spoke of his mother, her frequent requests and pleas crowded his mind in an instant and his voice choked on sobs.

Adhar said, 'If you want to burn your Maa, get five rupees as the price of the tree. Can you get it?'

Kaangaali knew this was impossible. He had seen that Bindi's aunt had gone to pawn the little brass plate from which he ate rice for one rupee to buy his *uttariya*[14]. So he shook his head and said, 'No.'

Adhar twisted his face and said, 'If no, go and bury your

---

[13]This is the ritual of sprinkling water mixed with cow dung.
[14]Upper robe

Maa on the river bank. How dare your Baap[15] put an axe to a tree—does it belong to his Baap? Wicked, worthless!'

Kaangaali pleaded, 'But babumoshai, it grows in our courtyard. My mother had planted it with her own hands.'

'Planted with her own hands! Parhey, chuck him out by the scruff of his neck!'

Parhey came and flung him out by the scruff of his neck, and uttered such words of abuse only the office-bearers of the zamindar knew how to utter.

Kaangaali stood up and dusted himself. Then he slowly left the place. The boy could not think of any reason as to why he had been beaten, where he was at fault. The gomostah's indifferent mind did not even register the incident. If it had the power to do so, he would not have got this job. He said, 'Paresh, just check and see if the fellow has any taxes due. If there is, just go and grab his fishing net or something—the bastard might run away.'

The funeral rites of the shraddh was just one day away in the Mukhujje household. The preparations were on a scale befitting the mistress of the house. Old Thakurdas was supervising everything himself: Kaangaali came and stood before him. He said, 'Thakurmoshai, my Maa is dead.'

'Who are you? What do you want?'

'I'm Kaangaali. My Maa wanted fire from my hands.'

'So go give it.'

The incident at the kacheri had spread quite quickly. Somebody said, 'Perhaps he wants a tree.'

Mukhujje was surprised and angry, 'Listen to him! I myself need so much wood, the shraddh is the day after tomorrow.

---

[15]A rough, colloquial reference to someone's father.

Go, go, there is nothing for you here, just nothing for you.'
He then went off elsewhere.

Bhattacharya-babu was preparing a list a little way off; he commented, 'In your caste, who has ever burnt a corpse? Go, light a bit of straw and touch it to her lips and bury her on the river bank.'

The eldest son of Mukhopadhyay was going somewhere, he paused a bit, heard the exchange intently, and then commented, 'See Bhattacharya-moshai, all chaps want to be either Bamuns or Kayeths.' He then hurried away, bowed under the pressure of work.

Kaangaali stopped pleading. These two hours of exposure to the ways of the world had turned him into an old man. In silence and taking slow steps, he went and stood by his mother's dead body.

Abhaagi was laid out in the hole dug near the river bank. Rakhal's mother placed a blazing sheaf of straw in his hand, and helped him to hold it to his mother's lips, and then threw it away. Then everyone helped to shovel the earth into the grave and thus obliterated all signs of Kaangaali's mother.

Everyone was very busy. Only Kaangaali remained still, his gaze—unblinking—turned towards the little plume of smoke spiraling skywards, curling out from the burnt sheaf of straw.

twelve

EKADASHI BAIRAGI[*]

*K*alidaha is primarily a Brahmin-dominated village. Gopal Mukhujje's son, Apurba, had always been the leader of the boys there. Now that he had returned home after a stint of five to six years in a Calcutta hostel and had cleared his BA with an Honours, his influence and power within his village became limitless. The village boasted of a dilapidated high school. Apurba's erstwhile playmates had curtailed their studies in this ramshackle building, had abandoned the Brahminic evening rituals, and were now busily acquiring the latest styles in haircuts. When the Calcutta-returned 'graduate'[1] unabashedly displayed an old-fashioned close-crop, with a thick tuft flush in the middle of his head, not just the youthful population but even their progenitors were dumbstruck.

During his stay in Calcutta, Apurba had acquired the membership of various *sabha*s and *samiti*s[2], and had attended

---

[*]Translated from the original with the same title, in *SSS*, Vol. 1, pp. 779–84.
[1]Saratchandra used the English word.
[2]Committees and associations

the lectures of the cognoscenti. He was, therefore, chock-full of abstruse knowledge about the esoteric mysteries of the Sanatana Hindu dharma, and he launched forth upon a full-throated, fulsome panegyric of the excellence of the traditional dharma. Its wonderfully systematic rituals were based on modern science. The tuft was a wonderful conductor of electricity, the evening rituals were essential for sound health, green bananas created a beneficial chemical reaction within the body and many other facts—unheard of—were revealed to one and all. Old and young men were equally bedazzled, and the result was that very soon tufts became highly fashionable and visible, while even the women of these households were beaten hands down by the men in the diligent observance of evening rituals, of *ekadashi*, of *purnima*, and in ritual bathing in the Ganges. The entire youth population was galvanized into programmes for the complete rejuvenation of the Hindu dharma as well as the nation. The old men sagely began to say, 'Yes, Gopal Mukhujje has some luck. Not only does the Goddess of fortune look kindly upon him, even his offspring is exceptional! Otherwise, how is it that in this day and age, and while still so young, and after passing as many English examinations, he is so deeply committed to the Hindu dharma?' Hence, Apurba became the cynosure of all eyes in his village. The three mettlesome and meddlesome associations that sprang up under Apurba's leadership—*Hindudharma Pracharini, Dhumpaan Nibarani*, and *Durnitidalani*[3]—began to make their presence felt even amongst the peasants. Thus, when word got around that Panchkodi Tewar beat up his wife under the influence

---

[3]The Association for the spread of Hinduism; The Association for Banning Smoking; The Association for Crushing Bad Ethics

of too much toddy, Apurba arrived forthwith with his gang. They disciplined Panchkodi so rigorously that the very next day his wife ran away with Panchkodi to her father's house. Bhaga Kaora was returning home very late at night from the river with a catch of fish, and high on ganja, venting raucous renditions of Malini's songs from 'Vidyasundar'[4]. These caught the ears of Abinash from the Brahmin neighbourhood, and he only let Bhaga go after bloodying his nose. The fifteen or sixteen–year-old son of Durga Dom was smoking a *bidi* as he was walking through the village field. A member of Apurba's gang spotted him smoking and put out the burning bidi on his back, thus raising blisters. In such a manner did Apurba's *Hindudharma Pracharini* and *Durnitidalani* associations erupt in Kalidaha village and like Bhanumati's[5] magical trees, bore fruits and flowers instantly. Now, Apurba turned his attention towards the intellectual improvement of his village. He was horrified to discover that in the school library, barring one and a half maps of Shashibhushan, and two and a half novels of Bankimchandra, there was nothing else. He humiliated the headmaster no end for this paucity, and then gearing himself up, he finally decided to build the library up himself. Under his presidentship, there was no delay in drawing up rules and regulations, the list of books and the donation notebook of the future library.

The villagers had managed to withstand the enthusiastic

---

[4]Bharat Chandra wrote the long poem 'Vidyasundar' in the eighteenth century, and it was considered very vulgar in the reformed Bengali cultural milieu of the nineteenth century, as many passages were considered improperly erotic. Malini's songs were very risque as she was the go-between of the young lovers in the poem—Vidya and Sundar.

[5]Bhanumati is a legendary sorceress in Bengali folklore.

religious reforms of the youth with equanimity. But within a day or two, their enthusiasm for collecting subscriptions became so terrifying for the rich and poor households alike, that doors and windows slammed shut the moment anyone spotted the approach of young men with notebooks tucked under their arms. It was clear that the path towards donations for a library was not even a fraction of the broad highway that had greeted religious reforms and the reform of evil habits. Apurba was getting very worried over this obstacle, when suddenly a very simple solution presented itself. Apurba had spotted an abandoned homestead a little way away from the school. He learned upon enquiry that it belonged to Ekadashi Bairagi. Further, that some ten years ago, the village Brahmins had disallowed him the services of the washerman, the barber and the grocer, and had banished him from the village, forcing him to migrate to another village for a heinous social crime. Now he lived some two krosh away in another village called Baruipur. He was reputed to be a wealthy shark; but nobody remembered this miser's real name—owing to the fear of experiencing a day of misfortune without food[6], it had completely faded from people's memories through sheer disuse. Since then, Bairagi-*mohashoyey* was known only as *Ekadashi*. Apurba beat a quick tattoo with his fingers and declared, 'A moneyed shark! Social crime! Then this is the fellow who can be forced to bear half the cost of the library. If not, the services of the washerman, the barber, and the grocer will stop

---

[6]'Haandi phaata' (as is used in the original) is a colloquial expression that connotes the ill-luck a miser brings if one chances to see him. It was believed that that meeting would prevent cooking that day.

there too! The zamindar of Baruipur is my mama–swasoor.'[7]

The young men became jubilant and a huge amount of money was entered against Ekadashi Bairagi's name in the notebook right away. Rasik Smritiratna heard the news that Ekadashi Bairagi would be forced to disgorge a huge amount of money for the library, and if he should prove obdurate, Apurba would ensure that the services of the washerman, the barber and the grocer would be stopped in Baruipur too. As a well-wisher of the library, he advised Apurba and his gang to extract a fat sum, failing which the Bairagi should be pressed to part with his own property in Kalidaha. Smritiratna was well aware that even though Bairagi did not reside on his patch of paternal property, he was very attached to it. Some two years ago, Smritiratna had wanted to buy this bit of land to round off his own orchard, but in spite of all his efforts, he had not been successful. When he had first broached the subject, Bairagi had put his hands to his ears, and like an extremely honest and humble man, had said, 'Please, there is no need for a deal, Thakurmoshai. I cannot think of taking money from a Brahmin for that little bit of land. That it will be of some service to a Brahmin is my good fortune accruing (to me) from seven generations.' Smritiratna had been thrilled to the core and blessed him and his sense of respect for the Gods and Brahmins a million, a zillion number of times. After this gush of feeling had petered out, Ekadashi had folded his hands together and with great humility, added the rider, 'But, Thakurmoshai, such is my misfortune, that there is no way I can part with this paternal property handed down over seven generations. My father, with his dying breath had said,

---

[7]Elder sister's father-in-law

"even if you do not have money for food, do not sell this old homestead", et cetera, et cetera.' Smritiratna had not forgotten his fury at being baulked in such a manner.

One morning, some five days later, a band of young men walked the necessary two krosh and arrived at Ekadashi's main gate. It was a mud-house, but very clean and tidy, and hinted at Lakshmi's presence. Neither Apurba nor any of his cronies had ever set eyes on Ekadashi. But now that they saw him, they all felt repelled by his personality and appearance. This man might have been a moneyed shark, but it was certain he would not contribute even a single small-fry to the library fund. Ekadashi was a moneylender by profession. He was over sixty years of age. His body was dry and shrivelled. His neck was covered in tulsi beads. He was clean shaven, and when one looked at his face, it did not look like he possessed even a trace of emotion. Like the rind of the sugarcane—after all the juice has been squeezed out by the press—becomes the fuel to burn the dry rind, this individual would in the same manner wring out and sacrifice all his humaneness to burn people as a moneylender. Just looking at him made Apurba demotivated. On the *Chandimandap*[8] an expanse of bedding was spread out. In the centre, sat Ekadashi. In front of him was a wooden chest. Next to him was a stack of papers. An elderly, bare-bodied gomostah was bent over a slate, working out amounts of interest. His sacred thread dangled from his neck. In front, on the sides, leaning on fence posts around the verandah, were seated glum-faced men and women of all ages and from different walks of life. Some had come to

---

[8]The village public space used by influential local men before the goddess's sanctum sanctorum.

borrow money, some to pay interest, some had just come to beg for a little more time. But from a cursory examination of the faces, it did not appear that there were people who had come to repay their debts.

Ekadashi was surprised at the sudden appearance of these unknown and respectable young men. The gomostah laid aside his slate and asked, 'Where are you from?'

Apurba replied, 'From Kalidaha.'

'And who are you?'

'We are all Brahmins.'

Ekadashi rose respectfully, bent forward in greeting when he heard they were Brahmins, and urged, 'Please be seated.'

After everyone had seated themselves, Ekadashi too sat down. The gomostah inquired, 'What is your purpose here?'

Apurba initiated his request for funds for the library with a brief outline about its usefulness, but he suddenly observed that Ekadashi Bairagi's head had swivelled towards the direction of a woman sitting behind a pillar, and he was saying, 'Have you run mad, Haru's mother? The interest has amounted to 7 rupees 2 annas[9], and you want 2 annas to be taken off the total? It will be kinder if you place your foot on my neck and murder me outright.'

Straightaway, the two embarked upon such a tug of war over 2 annas that seemingly their lives hung in the balance over the outcome. If Haru's mother was resolute, Ekadashi was equally unrelenting. Apurba intervened between the two combatants, for he was getting late, 'The matter about our library—'

Ekadashi turned his head a little and said, 'Indeed, yes,

[9]One anna equals 4 paise. There are 16 annas in a rupee.

in a little bit, sir—oh yes, Nafar! Do you want to drown me by putting your foot on my head, hey? You have not yet returned that two-rupee loan, and now, shamelessly you ask for a rupee more? Say, have you at least got the interest for the previous loan?'

When Nafar opened the sling at his waist and produced an anna, Ekadashi demanded angrily, 'Haven't three months passed by? Why isn't there 2 paise more?'

Nafar, with folded hands, begged, 'Karta, there isn't any more. I just managed to beg these 4 paise from Dhada's son. I will return the remaining 2 paise, after the forthcoming fair is over.'

Ekadashi stretched out his neck and said, 'Let me see the other sling.'

Nafar opened the sling on the left side and said in a hurt voice, 'Am I lying for 2 paise Karta? Death on the fellow who brings the money and still tries to cheat you, I say.'

Ekadashi's gaze became sharp—'You managed to borrow 4 paise, and you couldn't borrow 2 paise more?' Nafar said angrily, 'Didn't I just swear that I haven't got it, Karta? May death seize me if I am lying.'

Apurba was seething with rage, and now he burst into uncontrollable speech: 'You are a fine one, Mister!'

Ekadashi merely glanced at him, but did not vouchsafe an answer. Instead, he beckoned to Paran Baagdi who was crossing the verandah, and said, 'Just open his waistband to see if he has the 2 paise hidden away there?'

The moment Paran came up, Nafar hastily untied his waistband, and flung the 2 paise before Ekadashi. Ekadashi was not at all affected by such insolence. He picked up the 6 paise with a straight face, and told the gomostah, 'Please enter 6 paise in Nafraa's name. And what are you going to do with another rupee—hey?'

Nafar said, 'I wouldn't have come if I didn't need it.'

Ekadashi said, 'Why don't you take 8 annas? You will fling away money if you take a whole rupee.'

After a lot of bargaining, Nafar Mandal managed a further loan of 12 annas.

The day was getting on. Anaath, a companion of Apurba, threw the notebook for donations in front of Ekadashi and said, 'Just give what you want, we cannot wait forever.'

Ekadashi picked up the notebook, examined it closely for a good fifteen minutes, finally heaved a sigh and said, 'I am an old man, why ask me for donations?'

With supreme effort, Apurba controlled his temper, and said, 'It is more fitting that old men give money, rather than young boys—for boys normally do not have any money.'

The old man did not reply to this, but instead remarked, 'There has been a school for the last twenty to twenty-five years. I haven't heard anyone bring up the issue of the library before this. Oh well, this is not a bad thing, and even if our children do not get to read the books, the village boys will at least read them, right? What do you say Ghoshal-moshai?' The nature of Ghoshal's reply, with an accompanying shake of the head, was not quite clear, but Ekadashi continued: 'Oh well, I will subscribe to the library; come back one of these days and take 4 annas from me. Any amount lesser than this does not look good, eh—Ghoshal? What do you say? The boys have come to me from such a distance only because I am reasonably well known in these parts. There are other people, too, but the boys have not gone to them with their request, right? What do you say?'

Apurba could not speak out of sheer rage. Anaath took up the slack, 'We have come so far for just 4 annas? That too we have to collect some other day?'

Ekadashi clicked his tongue, and said, sadly shaking his head, 'You yourselves witnessed the situation here. Even for 6 annas, one has to really go after these chaps. It is an inconvenient time for donations until this season's jute is sold—.' Apurba, his lips trembling with anger, said, 'It will be convenient when the services of the washerman and the barber are stopped here too. Bloody vampire, decked up in Vaishnav marks all over after losing caste—very nice!'

Bipin stood up and lifted a finger threateningly—'Keep in mind that the zamindar of Baruipur is our relative, Bairagi!'

The old Bairagi looked on helplessly at this unthinkable turn of events. The reason for this burst of wrath on the part of these strangers from a different village escaped him entirely. Apurba said, 'I will make sure you do not get another chance to extract interest and suck the poor people's blood dry.'

Nafar was still sitting there. He was still seething with the extraction of the 2 paise from his waistband. He said, 'Karta, what you said is quite right. He is not a Bairagi, he is a vampire! You saw with your own eyes how he took 2 paise from me.'

Everyone present was experiencing pure happiness at this humiliation of the old man. Bipin noticed their expressions and enthusiastically winked and said slyly, 'You do not know the inside story, but we come from his old village, we know all. So, old man, shall we tell why the services of the washerman and the barber were forbidden to you in our village?'

It was old news. Everyone knew it. Ekadashi was a Sadgop by caste, not a Vaishnav. But when his only stepsister left their *kula*[10] under the compelling temptation of youthful desires, Ekadashi managed to track her whereabouts and bring her back home, even though it was not an easy task and he underwent much hardship. But this deliberate social misdeed both surprised and angered the villagers. However, Ekadashi could not abandon this little orphaned stepsister of his, even under such social pressure. He had no one else to call his own. He had brought her up since childhood, and had, with much fanfare, given her away in marriage. When she was widowed at a tender age, she came back to her brother's house, to the familiar love and care. The old man wept bitterly when his much beloved little sister committed a grave social error out of youthful ignorance. He proscribed food and sleep, trudged through village after village, town after town, and at last located her and returned home with her. He was unable to accept the cruel dictum of the villagers and expel his deeply ashamed, repentant, and unfortunate little sister—and keep himself safely within his caste with ritualistic penance. Thus the services of the washerman, the barber and other services were closed for him in the village. Therefore, Ekadashi became a Vaishnav, as there was no other way to survive, and escaped to Baruipur. All knew the story, but it was sweeter to hear scandalous tales about other people, and everyone waited with bated breath for more sordid revelations. But Ekadashi became a bundle of shame and fear all at once—not for himself but for his little sister. Gouri still suffered intense mental agonies from the error committed in the first flush of youth. The old man knew well that this wound was as raw and unhealed as when she had first suffered under its lash. Ekadashi, certain that the

---

[10]Family

old pain would stir into acute life at even a hint of gossip, looked on in mute anxiety. His piteous look of appeal escaped everyone else's attention, but suddenly Apurba sensed it and was struck dumb with amazement.

Bipin, however, was in full career, 'Are we beggars that we have travelled for over two krosh for 4 annas? And we have to come another day for his bounty, when his debtor would have sold his jute—we have to walk all the way again in the hope that the Babu will be pleased to be kind? But do you think, you bloodsucking old man, that a leech is safe from another leech? If I do not make this village too hot for you, my name is not Bipin Bhattacharya. You, a low caste, are so blinded by your money? Come on, Apurba, let's go, we will then do—you know what.' And he gave Apurba's hand a tug.

By now, it was past eleven. Apurba had asked a servant some time ago to bring some water as he had felt intensely thirsty after walking such a long way. He had forgotten his request in the heat of battle. However, when a twenty-seven to twenty-eight-year-old young woman came in from a side door with a glass of water in one hand and some sugar crystals in a bowl held in the other, he remembered his request. Gouri did not appear to have been born into a low caste. She was wearing a *garad*[11] sari. She had just seated herself to offer ritual oblations to the deity, but had abandoned her duty to the family god the instant a servant had conveyed a Brahmin's request for water. She now inquired very politely, 'Who amongst you required water?'

Bipin returned roughly, 'Just because you are wearing a silk sari, do you suppose we shall take water from your hands?

---

[11]Undyed silk

Hey Apurba, this is that female!'

The bowl of sugar crystals fell with a crash on the floor from the young woman's hand, and Apurba himself suffered intense embarrassment and shame when he glimpsed boundless shame in another pair of eyes. He angrily nudged Bipin with his elbow, and said, 'You have lost all sense of proportion—what are you saying?'

Bipin was an impartial, brave villager, for he did not differentiate between the male and the female of the species in the face of a quarrel. His cruelty increased under Apurba's nudge. He raised his voice even further and challenged, 'Why, am I saying anything wrong? She dares to bring water for a Brahmin? Do you know I can spill many things in public?'

Apurba realized that further argument was useless. Bipin would merely become more insulting. He therefore said, 'I had requested for some water, Bipin, there is no need to be annoyed. Come, let's go.'

Gouri picked up the bowl, and retreated behind a door without another glance at anyone. From there she asked, 'Dada, have you given these gentlemen the donation that they had requested?'

Ekadashi had been sitting like one totally bewildered, but now he sat up at his sister's address, and said, 'No, I am about to do so, didi.'

He then looked at Apurba, and with folded hands, appealed to him, 'Babumoshai, I am a poor man. Kindly receive 4 annas from me, and believe me, it is a lot for me.'

Bipin was about to explode again, but Apurba signalled him to hold his peace. But he himself felt deeply contemptuous of the proposed donation of 4 annas, after such a prolonged and charged contretemps had taken place. Yet he restrained himself and said quietly, 'Never mind, Bairagi, you do not have to give anything at all.'

Ekadashi understood that this was not in a kind spirit. He heaved a sigh, and said, '*Kalikal!*[12] Nobody can resist the temptation to break someone's neck if the opportunity presents itself. All right, Ghoshal-moshai, write down 5 annas as expenditure in the book. What else can I do, tell me.' Bairagi then heaved another huge sigh. This time Apurba, glancing at his face, felt like laughing. He fathomed that to this old man who lived for interest alone, there was a vast gulf between 4 annas and 5 annas. He smiled slightly and said, 'It is all right, you don't have to give anything at all. We do not take 5 annas as donation. We are leaving.'

For some reason, Apurba had expected some form of protest to come from behind the door. The end of Gouri's sari could still be seen but no word came from there. As he prepared to leave, Apurba thought with true sadness, 'Indeed, these people are very petty. They live for money alone, they cannot think beyond 5 annas for donation. Money is their life, their flesh and bone, there is nothing in the world they cannot do for money.'

As Apurba got up with his gang, Anaath's eyes fell on a small boy of about ten. He had a long, white uttariya around his neck; possibly he had suffered the death of his father, or a similar bereavement. His widowed mother was sitting behind a pillar on the verandah. Anaath was surprised, and he asked, 'Puntey, what are you doing here?'

---

[12]The last phase in cyclical time when the material world is deeply corrupted, awaiting temporal renewal. The four phases of time are Satya, Treta, Dwapar and Kali.

Puntey pointed to his mother with his finger, 'My mother is here.' His mother said, 'We have a lot of money saved up with him,' and she indicated Ekadashi.

Everyone present felt both amazement and curiosity. Even Apurba felt the desire to see what finally came of it all, and despite his deep thirst, caught hold of Bipin's hand and both resumed their seats.

Ekadashi asked, 'Baba, what is your name? Where do you live?'

The little boy answered, 'My name is Sasadhar. My house is in their village—in Kalidaha.'

'And what is your father's name?'

Anaath answered for the boy, 'His father has passed away, it's been many years. His grandfather, Ramlocchan Chattujje, had left all familial ties after the death of his son and had disappeared. He had returned a month ago after seven years. But the day before yesterday, their house caught fire, and the old man died trying to put out the flames. There is nobody else; this little grandson has to perform the funeral rites.'

Hearing the story, everyone expressed their sympathies, except Ekadashi who kept silent. After a little while, he enquired, 'Is there a hundi[13] for the cash? Go and ask your mother.'

The boy returned with the answer, 'There was nothing—all papers and documentary evidence got burnt in the fire.'

Ekadashi asked, 'How much money?'

Now, the widow came forward, drew aside the end of the sari from her head, and said, 'Before he died, Thakur told us that he had entrusted 500 rupees for safekeeping before

---

[13]A form of credit instrument or IOU.

leaving for his pilgrimage. Baba, we are very poor, even if you do not give us all the money, give us some as charity.' So saying, the widow began to weep silently. Ghoshal-moshai had abandoned his account-keeping a long time ago and was listening to this exchange with great interest. Now, he came forward and asked, 'Are there any witnesses?'

The widow shook her head and said, 'No. Even we did not know. Thakur had secretly entrusted the money for safekeeping before leaving for his pilgrimage.'

Ghoshal-moshai smiled slightly, and said, 'Just crying here will not help. It is a matter of a lot of money; there is no handbill, no witnesses, how can the claim be taken seriously?'

The widow heaved with her sobs, but everyone present could guess how the matter would end. Now Ekadashi spoke once more. He looked at Ghoshal and said, 'I seem to remember somebody had left 500 rupees, and never came back to claim it. Why don't you look through some old books and see if there are any entries?'

Ghoshal snapped, 'Who is going to go through such a lot of work in the middle of the day? There are no witnesses, no handbills—'

Before he could finish his sentence, from behind the door came a sharp rejoinder, 'Just because there are no handbills or documentary evidence, will the Brahmin's money sink? Look at the old books, and if you are unable to do so, give them to me, I will.'

Everyone looked in amazement at the door, but the speaker could not be seen.

Ghoshal replied in a softer tone, 'Maa, so many years have elapsed. It will not be easy to find out the correct book. There are heaps of records. But, if it has been entered into the savings account, of course it will be found.' He then addressed the widow, 'Do not cry dear. If the claim is right, then of course you will receive the money. All right, why don't you come to my house tomorrow morning? I will get all the details from you, find out the right book and retrieve whatever has been entered. Today, it is very late, and nothing is possible.'

The widow agreed to this proposal immediately, and said, 'All right, baba, I will come to your place tomorrow morning.'

'Do so,' said Ghoshal and shut the books for the day.

But Ghoshal's strategy of summoning the widow for further questioning to his house was instantly crystal clear to everybody. However, Gouri spoke again from behind the door, 'It all happened eight years ago—why don't you see the books of the year 1301 BS, and check if the sum has been entered?'

Ghoshal asked, 'Maa, what's the hurry?'

Gouri replied, 'Very well, give the books to me, I shall look it up. A Brahmin's daughter has walked all of two krosh, she will walk back yet another two krosh, she will come again at your place tomorrow: is there any need for such an imbroglio, Ghoshal uncle?'

Ekadashi supported his sister, 'Indeed Ghoshal-moshai. It is not good to compel a Brahmin's daughter to do so much running around needlessly. Goodness, no! Come come, look it up quickly.'

The angry Ghoshal got up in a rage, and from the next room retrieved the accounts book maintained in 1301 BS. He turned over the pages for some ten minutes, and then suddenly, in a very pleased voice, said, 'Wonderful! My Gouri-maa's intelligence is really remarkable! The entry has been made in the very year's accounts book she indicated. Here it is! The entry of 500 rupees against Ramlochan Chattujje's name!'

Ekadashi said, 'Now quickly work out the interest on it, Ghoshal-moshai.'

Ghoshal was amazed, 'Even the interest?'

Ekadashi said, 'Of course, it has to be given. The money has been rolling for so many years. The interest for eight years—only these few months will not be counted.'

The entire amount, with the capital and the interest, came close to 750 rupees. Ekadashi addressed his sister, 'Didi, then take out the sum from the chest. So dear, will you take the whole amount at once?'

The All-knowing had listened to the widow's prayer from the heart. She wiped her eyes and then said, 'No, baba, I do not need so much money. Give me just 50 rupees for now.'

Ekadashi replied, 'Very well maa. Ghoshal-moshai, give me the book once, let me sign it: in the meanwhile, you draw up a handbill for the rest of the money.'

Ghoshal said, 'I can sign, it is not necessary for you—'

Ekadashi said, 'No, no, give it to me, let me just check with my own eyes.' He took the book, ran his eyes over it for half a minute, then smiled and said, 'Ghoshal-moshai, here, there are a pair of real pearls entered against the Brahmin's name. I happen to know that our Thakurmoshai cannot see things with his eyes sometimes.' So saying, Ekadashi looked towards the door with a little smile. Ghoshal's face darkened at his employer's sarcastic statement in front of so many people.

When all the work for that day had been completed, and Apurba finally stepped out into the burning road with his companions, there was a revolution raging in his mind. Ghoshal was accompanying them, and he issued an invitation to them all with great humility, 'Please, step into my poor home; have at least a bit of jaggery with water.'

Apurba wordlessly followed everyone else. Ghoshal's anger was consuming him. He said, referring to Ekadashi, 'Did you witness the insolence of a *chhotolok*[14] like him? It is the good fortune of his last sixteen generations that the dust from the feet of such Brahmin children like you have purified his home. The fellow is a vampire in that he wants to get rid of beggars at the door with 5 annas!'

Bipin reassured him, 'Wait for a couple of days. We will stop the bastard's washerman-barber services here too so that he can indeed repent for his offer of 5 annas as subscription. Please keep in mind that Rakhal-babu is our relative, Ghoshal-moshai.'

Ghoshal said, 'I am a Brahmin. I do not touch water without performing my Brahminic rituals twice a day, and you saw how the fellow insulted me at high noon over a couple of trumpery pearls! He will never prosper! Don't even think it! And that female—you have to take a bath if you happen to touch her—actually comes with water to quench a Brahmin's thirst! Just think how insolent they have become just because they have money!'

Apurba had, so far, not contributed a single word to the conversation. He suddenly halted in the middle of the road and said, 'Anaath, *bhai*, I have to return, I am very thirsty.'

Ghoshal was surprised, 'But my house is just here, why will you go back?'

Apurba shook his head and said, 'Please, you take the others to your house, I am going to the house of Ekadashi to drink water.'

Going to Ekadashi's house to drink water! Everyone

---

[14]A lowlife

abruptly stopped in shocked surprise, and their eyes rolled up to the middle of their foreheads. Bipin gave his hand a tug, and said, 'Come on, you don't have to play-act in the middle of the road at high noon. Of course you are just the person to go and drink the water touched by Ekadashi's sister!'

Apurba pulled his hand away and said firmly, 'Indeed, I am going back just to drink that water she has touched. You lot have some food at Ghoshal-moshai's place. I will wait for you under this tree.'

At his calm, collected voice, Ghoshal, completely bewildered, said, 'But do you know you will have to do penance for this?'

Anaath asked, 'Have you gone mad?'

Apurba said, 'Do I not know it? But I can take all the time in the world over the penance. Yet right now I cannot wait,' and quickly began retracing his steps to Ekadashi's house under the burning sun.

ACKNOWLEDGEMENTS

This collection of translation owes much to the wonderful space and camaraderie I received at the Indian Institute of Advanced Study, Shimla, and my deepest thanks go to Chetan Singh, K.L. Tuteja, Aryak, Kaustav, Esha, Albina, Sukumar, Soumya and Uma. To Arvind, Aparna, Pranav, Sheela, Sasheej, Sanjay Subodh, Sanjay Palshikar and Raja in the University of Hyderabad—special thanks are due for their insightful observations on Saratchandra. And of course to Pramod Nayar—expressing thanks with interest. And to Rinita of Rupa—not just for great copyediting, but for reading Saratchandra for me.

Heartfelt thanks to Subir Mitra of Ananda Publications for being reassuring about my using *Sulabh Sarat Samagra*, volumes 1 and 2, for this collection.

To my students Saptarshi and Ashesh—for listening with such attentive ears to the translated word, arguing about the right word, and helping so much with the editing. They were my first readers and their response encouraged me to think that Saratchandra still spoke to young minds. To Dada, who always responded to my computer issues amid hectic schedules.

To Mamoni for holding the fort, as always. To Puchki too, for snoring through it all.